The King ...

A
Desert
Adventure

King Camel. Copyrights 2014 (Copr.) Boy and the Camel Series. Maximus Basco - MARS Productions Corp. Miami, Florida. All rights reserved. Printed in the United States. No part of this book may be used or reproduced in any manner whatsoever without rewritten permission except in the case of brief quotations or embodied in critical articles and/or reviews.

For information about reproduction, printing or copyrights for alternative media outlets please contact us via email at maximusbasco@gmail.com

FIRST EDITION 2014
ILLUSTRATION BY MAXIMUS BASCO. ISBN-13: 978-1503083462

United States Copyrights Office.

The following files were successfully uploaded for service request 1-1874446171 - Boy and The Camel Illustrated

This book may be bought at Createspace.com and/or Amazon.com as hardcopy or as an electronic book for Tablets, iPads, and related reading electronic devices for educational purposes at a discounted price.

Dedication

This book is dedicated to my son who inspired me to write; not only by believing in me but sharing with me his beautiful childhood dream about the talking camel. It gave form to characters and plots around which the story of Peter and Sarah revolves.

The White Talking Camel is as much his fantasy as is of this writer. I also dedicate this book to all members of the family who in one way or another have always encouraged me to pursue my writer's aspirations.

And of course, I dedicate this bedtime story to all members of my family, who have equally believe in this project and supported me throughout patiently. I've taken hundreds of hours from family time to complete this book; for that, I thank each of them.

I thank friends who read the raw manuscript and encouraged me to better this project with valuable suggestions. I dedicate King Camel be time story to all children of the world hoping these storylines bring them happiness to them as they read.

I especially think of my grandchildren, Nicole, Daniel, Gianna, and Tristen who may read it in the near future *and travel with Peter and Sarah to Egypt and meet the White Talking Camel themselves.*

Maximus Basco/MARS

Chapters

- **Chapter One - A Letter from Father**
- **Chapter Two - A Camel King**
- **Chapter Three - The Trip to Egypt –**
- **Chapter Four - Bedtime Stories –**
- **Chapter Five - On the Castle-One-**
- **Chapter Six – Hercules Pillars**
- **Chapter Seven - The Thieves**
- **Chapter Eight – Desert Kidnap**
- **Chapter Nine - The Talking Camel**
- **Chapter Ten - New Destination**
- **Chapter Eleven - The Escape Plan**
- **Chapter Twelve - Entering Khufu**
- **Chapter Thirteen - Giggling Marbles**
- **Chapter Fourteen - Cairo Escape**
- **Chapter Fifteen - The Beggar's Gold**
- **Chapter Sixteen – Ambitious Beggar**
- **Chapter Seventeen - The Cook**
- **Chapter Eighteen - A Mathematician**
- **Chapter Nineteen - Grant Me One Wish**
- **Chapter Twenty - Grand-Oasis**
- **Chapter Twentyone Final Destination**
- **Chapter Twentytwo - Goes Home**
- **Twenty-Three - A New King**

Chapter One
A Letter from Father

Peter and Sarah jumped out quickly from the horse carriage. London's sky seemed bluer than ever for Springtime had returned to England again and flowers were bloomed everywhere while most of the trees turned leaving the cold of Wintertime.

Peter and Sarah walked with their mother to the Post Office to pick their father's letter.

The day felt warm as the soft afternoon sun rays fell over the city.

Everything around London seemed bright and lively. People crossed the streets from sidewalk to sidewalk while horse carriages trotted rapidly; their hooves clacking noisily London's cobblestone streets.

The children, holding to their mother's hands, went from the sidewalk up to the postal service inside London's Library. Peter climbed the stairs in quick steps in front of his mother and sister getting to the door before them.

Taller than his sister, and most boys his age, he looked a bit slim while Sarah seemed perhaps a bit plum; her reddish hair and hazel eyes put her on her mother's side. Peter seven just a few weeks ago, attended second grade while Sarah went to first grade for sounds and letters for six-year-olds. Both enjoy books and their parents reading bedtime stories for them.

Peter wore his favorite beige shorts today; his blue wool sweater and his dark shoes. His straight hair fell from his head straight to one side. I take after father, he proudly would say, if anybody asked.

Sarah in her white flowered dress and pink shoes ran after her brother going for the door. Her round face and grayish eyes came from her mother's side, she loved to say as well.

Peter got to the door before his mother and sister and opened it. The two children and their mother entered the old postal building to pick up their father's letter. The building's heavy, dark oak door protected by tall columns faced the busiest London's street.

Inside the postal services office, the old mail clerk, Mr. Bernard, sorted letters amongst other clerks like himself. They handed and sorted letters when the Carnehill family walked in looking for their letters. Peter and Sarah curiously glanced around as Mr. Bernard, a man of white hair and of ruddy cheeks looking a bit like Santa indeed said hello. Peter told his sister who looked like in a whisper and they giggled.

"He has puffy red cheeks and white hair and glasses like Papa Noel," Sarah said, and both giggled again. Mr. Bernard lifted his eyes and cheerfully greeted the family. He welcomed Mrs. Carnerhill and her children; the family of Mr. Maxwel Carnerhill, the English Ambassador in Egypt, he remembered.

"Good morning Mrs. Carnerhill," he said for he knew the family well for over a year when the Honorable Ambassador went to Egypt.

He lowered his blue, watery and sleepy eyes and pushed up the thick glasses perched on his nose, and said saying good morning to Peter and Sarah, greeting them also.

"Good afternoon Mr. Bernard," Mrs. Carnerhill replied politely and she asked her children to greet Mr. Bernard too. And both children cheerfully said, "good afternoon to you Mr. Bernard".

"Oh, please call me Ber. I never like this old and silly French name, he said, and he winked an eye and flared his nostrils to the children and grinned to them while doing his trick.

"He can flare his nostrils like a dragon! Peter whispered softly to Sarah. They giggled together but Peter remained perfectly still, straight and looking at the old man's nose; his slim frame like in military attention.

"Please do it again, Mr. Bernard," asked Peter as he pressed is hair perfectly cut and combed to one side.

"Can you do this like me? Mr. Bernard asked Peter, then asked Sarah flaring his nostrils like tiny wings. He smiled and fixed his skyblue eyes on Peter and on Sarah this time. Sarah hid behind her mother's skirt a bit shy perhaps, but soon she pushed her head sideways to see the old Mr. Bernard's flaring nostrils. Mr. Bernard flared his nostrils again gazing and wiggling at her.

"How about you Peter? Can you flare your nostrils like this? Pretend to be a friendly dragon, puffing balls of fire like in the old tales from Marlin the Wizard," he asked with a warm smile. The Children giggled again watching Mr. Bernard nostrils flaring up like the nose of a camel.

"Just pretend to be a flying dragon and flare your nose. Just twitch your nose," Mr. Bernard said with a grin on his friendly face looking like Santa Claus with glassed on his nose.

Peter tried hard. His nostrils never moved a twitch. He even pulled an earlobe to help himself a bit as the clerk suggested. But his nostrils never flared like Mr. Bernard's nostrils did. He could wiggle his nose and could twitch it like a honey-smelling-bear miles away, he said grinning to the children.

"You have to practice a lot more." Mr. Bernard said, and his eyes under his bushy, grayish eyebrows growing over his thick glasses grew even bigger.

"Oh, don't worry children I've practiced for sixty-five years long. It is only now I can twitch my nose like this and flare my nostrils like that. "Don't be disappointed for practice, practice makes the master, my dear," he said grinning and showing his teeth behind a thick white mustache.

A canopy of white hair over his lips gave him the looks of Santa Clause's face with an untrimmed mustache and puffy red cheeks. His nose trick delighted the children and they laughed and giggled. He wiggled it once more for them. He saw them smile again and then, he stopped his nose tricks and stood up.

He then walked a few feet behind his desk, looked up and pulled a letter from the wall. A wall looking like a giant beehive with many holes; big holes that enough to fit squirrels in them, Peter thought, but of course, only letters filled the squares on the wall and Mr. Bernard reached for a yellow, paper envelope. He read the name on it and handed the letter to Mrs. Carnerhill. It was for her; from her husband.

It came from the Ambassador to Egypt. The stamp on its backflip read in pencil markings, Cairo, Egypt 1864 Year of the Lord. Sender: Honorable Maxwell Carnerhill, Ambassador for the Royal Kingdom of England, Mr. Bernard reads aloud for the delight of the children.

"My mom is going to take us all to Egypt," Peter said with a glow sparkling in his eyes. His voice is lively as he never sounded ever before.

"That's a long, long way from London," Mr. Bernard said.

"I'm going with my mom and Peter too," Sarah's voice sounded happy saying that. Her grayish glowing gleeful eyes locked on Mr. Bernard's eyes.

"We're going to visit our father in Egypt. We're going to ride a camel too," Peter added.

"Me too," Sarah said.

"How wonderful for you two children, "Mr. Bernard said. The old man's eyes looking at them. He smiled and said.

"Uhmm, how wonderful, I would give a million pounds to travel if I were a rich man and see Egypt with you. And go to see the pyramids!
"Ride on a camel as a king!

The old man said. Mr. Bernard's eyes wandered into space. For a second, perhaps imagining himself with the children.

"Children we must go now, "Mrs. Carnerhill said.

She thanked the postal clerk ready to turn around on her heels for the door, but then Mr. Bernard called out the children's names saying, "Ahh, Peter and Sarah, do you know Egypt is far from England? Maybe thousands of miles you're going to sail. Do you know that? And do you know Egypt had many Pharaohs like kings in Spain and Queens in England? And do you know that one of them was a child like you only?

Both children stop in their way out and listened to the old postal clerk speaking to them.

"And of course," he added, "Egypt is the land of old pyramids too! And one cannot forget the river, the Nile! The longest of all rivers in the world! And it's there in Egypt for you to see! He went on. "Do you know there are Oasis of freshwater in the middle of nowhere? Palm trees grow around small ponds, do you know that? People and camels go there to drink water and rest under the trees in the middle of the desert. Oh, children! Children! How wonderful for you to go!

"We're going to sail on the Castle One, it's the new ship of the royal company! Peter said with more excitement about the English ship.

"Many days you're going to sail for sure," the old clerk Mr. Bernard replied.

"But it's the fastest ship, very fast and it's going to take us no more than a month to Egypt, that's what father says, "Peter quickly replied also standing taller than most seven years olds. His long legs seemed growing faster than most kids his age under his shorts.

"Ahh...Peter, your father has informed you well. Now pay attention. Many camels you're going to see in Egypt. But be aware for there is one that is very special! Yes, sir!

"He wanders everywhere and runs great distances from here to there any moment! He might be very close to you at any time, ahh, but you cannot see even he is very near there, Mr. Bernard said fixing is eyes filled with wonder on Sarah then on Peter too.

"I would like to see that camel! And ride on its back, "Peter said almost in a shout of excitement.

"Me too, "Sarah dared to say in her tiny voice. Her hazel eyes sparkled on her face adorned with tiny freckles like stars like glitter on her rosy cheeks.

"Ahh, very well Sarah you're brave also. Soon, I'm sure you two are going to ride a camel indeed. But, did your father tell you about the most mysterious of all camels in the desert? The one nobody but only children? The old mail clerk asked the kids in a whisper like in secrecy. He pinched softly Sarah's pinkish cheek and ruffled Peter's hair gently with one hand.

"No, but all camels are especial, father says," said Sarah timidly.

"He's right dear Sarah. They all walk long, long distances in the desert, and don't drink water for days and are loyal to their Masters. But children tell me did you ever hear of the White Talking Camel?

"No, never, "Peter said with wide eyes and his mind traveled like the wind; his imagination flew like desert sands in an instant. A White Talking Camel wow! He asked himself aloud.

"It's the most handsome of all the camels; he's strong and tall and grace he trots lifting his snout with pride as he steps over the sands like a General for Royal Armies."

"Wow, is it very, very tall?

"He is tall enough to see all around him, and believe me, this camel wanders through the desert and only children can see him! But hear this too now.

Only children who are kind and brave can see him, they say! Only children who are of good heart can ride on its back! Mr. Bernard said smiling.

"Like Richard the Lion King a brave warrior, father says." "and kind as well, children, kind as well remember that."

"Can he bite me? Sarah asked.

"Ahh, no...he's nothing like other camels for he's tamed and kind with children."

"Well, let me tell you about him. This camel wanders through the desert. And only children can see it! Hear this. Only children who believe can see him, they say! Only children especially children can ride on its back! Mr. Bernard said smiling. "Oh… that is the White Talking Camel indeed! He's the one camel, only children can ride on its back, the story says! The old man repeated again.

"Pay attention children and listen," Mr. Bernard said.

Chapter Two
A Camel King Too

"The King of Camels He is! He is also a prince in his own world. His fur as white as snow might be when you see him at night and of any color of the sands when seeing him at daylight. Its fur may even softly glow blueish hues with the moon's light. His honey-brown eyes are large and round, but even when you think he's sleeping he's awake looking at everything around you. His big eyes look like walnuts on his long snout and he might even wink an eye with thick long eyelashes if he wants to talk to you and say hello! Mr. Bernard said and went on to say more.

"When does come to the desert, Mr. Bernard," Sarah ask curiously again.

"Well, he walks and runs in the desert anytime! He goes from here to there and then to anywhere at the speed of light. He's a true free camel! Oh yes, listen to this. The story says there're children who swear that this camel even walks on air and its hooves never touch the sands," Mr. Bernard said in a whisper.

"Can he fly indeed, like birds, Mr. Bernard," Sarah asked surprised.

"Shsssssssssssssss, says nothing about that." He smiled and kept saying. "Ah, yes, but pay attention again. Nobody can see him or hear this camel. The story says that this is a unique camel indeed knowing many languages. A camel that talks like you and me, but nobody can hear. Only children can see and hear him, they say! Yes. Only those who are brave and kind of heart like you are children!

"Only those, of course, will get to see the White Talking Camel says this fairytale. The camel of Ali Baba in the old, old days this camel learned many languages from many men and now talks like you and me!

"Is he for real Mr. Bernard? Peter asked once more.

"But of course, my dear! Again, pay attention to this tale. For they say that this camel one day escaped from Ali-Baba's herd of a thousand camels. Yes! He did escape to the desert; he went to be free again for he valued his freedom more than anything. More than jewels and gold, more than food and water he values his freedom, "Mr. Bernard whispered the words like a secret between them.

Peter and Sarah stood without moving, not wanting to go anywhere, but only wanting to listen to Mr. Bernard's story. "Aaahh, for sure it's going to come to you, children. The White Talking Camel crosses the desert anytime from here to there, day or night, they say. I'm sure you're going to meet him when he wants to come to you," the postal clerk said.

"Where does come, Mr. Bernard?

"Ahh, children, children, the White Talking Camel is of the finest family. He is also a camel king from afar, from a faraway nation and from a million miles and many Constellations he flew one day. "Are you of a brave heart and kind? Of course, you are; then you're going to see him and I have no doubt he'll come to you, and to you, Sarah," Mr. Bernard said looking at the Carnerhill kids.

"I can't wait to go looking for this camel. We should leave today, look for him and ride on his back," Peter said enthused. Then, as if remembering something else, Mr. Bernard said again.

"But listen to me well children for many desert bandits are going to say to you, "Hey little kid and your sister! Come here, and you also come to me here! They could say it in a soft whisper.

"Here come and see my camel. Shhsssssss be quiet. This is the real White Talking Camel! Yes!

"Ride on it for three wishes but pay me now one coin of gold. Ohh…Children, children! Do not believe them! It's all a trick and be aware of liars!

"We won't listen to them, Mr. Bernard, right Sarah? Peter said asking his sister, and she nodded her head,

"There is only one camel like this, yes only one indeed. The one with the most shining white coat he is! He is tall and strong. If he were human, a prince or king he would be here! He is also smart and knows much about numbers and stars.

He knows of constellations and the history of many nations for he has traveled the Universe. Be aware in many languages he may also talk to you two!

"You might hear him talking in English and Portuguese saying good morning or bom dia! Then, he also may talk to you in French or Spanish. He might say to you "Bon jour talking in French or Buenos Dias talking to you in Spanish," Mr. Bernard said smiling at them.

"What's his name, Mr. Bernard? Sarah asked curiously in all her innocence.

"Oh, my dear children you are going to know when he comes to you the first time. He will lower his front legs for you to jump on his back. He's going to wink an eye and say "hello I'm the talking camel and this is my name you know but it's a secret now between you and me! And you're going to ride on its back like a Sultan prince, Peter! You're going to say the White Talking Camel has come to me!

"And you Sarah my dear, you are going to ride in this beautiful animal like an African queen! Mr. Bernard said with a smile, then winked an eye to the children's mom and both merrily laughed.

"Have you ever seen the White Camel, Mr. Bernard? Peter asked his voice filled with curiosity.

"Oh, no, for I've never traveled like you going to Egypt. And if I were to travel now, I would have to be a child like you. I would have to be kind and brave to ride on a camel.

"So, be brave and kind and go and find the White Talking Camel indeed, "the postal clerk said with a grin looking at Mrs. Carnerhill.

"C'mon children….we must go now for…Mr. Bernard our dear friend has letters to send. Perhaps places to dream about I'm sure. He'll tell us about the White Talking Camel the next time around.
Your father will send us another letter. We're going to come again. Mrs. Carnerhill said. She smiled at Mr. Bernard the mail clerk and friend.

Then, pulling her kids to the door they went saying their goodbyes. The children wanted to ask many questions about the White Talking Camel, but by then, their mother's hands pulled them to the door.

Outside Big Ben called London's time. Its musical chimes the children heard in wonder gazing at its tall tower. The old Ben's clock rose over the river Thames. Boats of fishermen went under old London's Bridge waters. The bells played the Westminster Quarters notes at exactly a quarter-hour before five o'clock.

Children, children! We need to go immediately. Their mother said with her children in tow. They all hurried to seek the street walking down quickly to call a horse carriage. When got in the carriage it was getting late for evening supper all over London.

Soon bedtime tales and stories would be read to the children before going to bed. Mrs. Carnerhill raised a waving hand and called a carriage; it stopped only a few feet from them and quickly she haggled a good traveling fair to pay and home they went away.

Its sky covered with many soft shades of blues and pale pinkish mauves. The sun seemed to hide and going away as if wanting to sleep too. The dome of the sky looked like dragging yellows and soft grayish clouds like a veil of air covering all.

All carriages had lit their beacons for drivers to see, their wicks fluttered lighting the streets. London's Bridge stood over the river and its yellow walls glowed on the water as horse-drawn carriages went from one end to the other of the bridge over the Thames river. The carriage crossed the bridge, then it went through a few narrow streets. Sometime later, the carriage stopped in front of a large mansion house.

The Carnerhill children jumped from the carriage and ran inside laughing. After supper, they wanted to get in bed soon. They wanted to fall asleep quickly to dream and dream of faraway places, they said. They wanted to dream of deserts and camels! Yes! They wanted to dream they played with many children around them. In their dream, they all could ride flying on camel's back and above over the desert!

In their dreams, they wanted to ride on the back of the White Talking Camel! The king of camels they were sure would come and be in their dreams. They hopped into bed quickly saying good night to their mom. They gave her a hug and they got a kiss from her going to sleep.

Chapter Three
The Trip to Egypt

The morning sun rays of Springtime fell over the city port of old Plymouth making it warm and bright. The Castle One ship was ready for its trip to Egypt, the land of many kings. The port's many merchants around offered their goods with loud voices for those travelers sailing to Egypt. It was a long, long voyage on the Mediterranean ocean a trip to the far land of ancient mummies of Pharaohs. A million and one sounds filled the port when the carriage arrived at the seaport of Plymouth. Peter jumped from the carriage before Sarah and his mom and stood in wonder looking at the Castle One. The ship waited for all its passengers to come aboard; its two tall smokestacks rose high. His eyes explored everything around him and then, he looked up at the ship again. It was anchored just a few yards from the edge of the waters; it looked taller and larger than Saint Paul's cathedral in London.

The ship's smokestack, taller than any of the tallest columns outside at the portal of the church, Peter thought as men carrying sacs and luggage went up the ramp to the deck. Peter measured its side and it

17

looked a hundred times larger than a Cricket field, Peter told to Sarah and his mom.

His eyes explored all about the market of the port where some children shouted London's news; they walked with London's daily newspapers on them while older boys peddled goods. Then, from nowhere two boys came to Peter and Sarah and one said, "Hello little Mister and hello little Princess! Please tell us what are your names? This is Mark and this is Sonny; I'm a King and him only a Prince." One said jokingly and left behind their loud guffaws!!! The taller of the two boys laughed then he bowed; the shorter one giggled and bowed quickly at them too as both laughed at the same time and left running. Peter and Sarah said nothing but giggled too as the two boys left behind and returned to merrily play with their friends around.

"They funny? Sarah said surprised.

"Perhaps playing with us," Peter said smiling.

"Uuh! It stinks a lot in this market," Sarah said.

"All markets stink a lot; pinch your nose like this," Peter said pinching his nose with two fingers and Sarah clipped her nose with too. She tried indeed to stop the stench of fish and both laughed but before long a loud hoot called all passengers aboard. Peter's eyes caught with a row of men, all carrying large sacs on their backs. They went on the ramp from the ground up to the deck and then back. "Mom, what do those men carry on their backs? Peter quickly asked.

"They carry food and coal to keep the boilers' fire up. The steam pushes the ship on the water you know," her mom explained.

Then, again the men walked up and down the went carrying, like big and strong busy ants, foods and goods for all aboard. The men walked up and down the plank each carrying suitcases or sacs. They went from the ground to the ship's hull above deck, up the ramp and others climbed down with plank, plank, plank noisy strides.

By then, their mother had paid the driver and he horse-carriage made its way out of the market.

The Carnerhill family stood behind ready to go onboard and got help from three men who came for their luggage and carried it away aboard the ship. The last hoot called all passengers to the ocean liner soon to leave the port of Plymouth. The ship was ready to go. It was ready for its way to the city of Alexandria in Egypt, the land kings, and Pharaohs.

"Look, Sarah, look up there! Peter said pointing to the white letters on the ship's hull. "Castle One," Peter read with pride and Sarah too tried to read each letter one by one.

Sarah did repeat after Peter.

"Castle-One it says, it's the ship's name," she said. She was happy to read it too. She was learning vowels and sounds. She wanted to read all the books anywhere in the world now that she put sounds together. She loved all books about Egypt and Pharaohs, she told Peter and she pointed to where passengers stood, all waving their goodbyes. Both children wanted to walk up the rail too, where people aboard were saying farewells to families on the ground.

"Children walk, walk children, "their mom said. They walked on the passengers' ramp-up to the boarding deck.

"To Egypt…wow! We're going to Egypt now Sarah!! Peter said smiling to his sister, his glowing with happiness as they went up the ship.

The ship hooted long and then loud one more time; it was ready to leave port. On the ship's final hoot, the ship moved slowly away from the waters while on the port below people yelled their goodbyes.

"Goodbye, adios amigos and ciao", they said. Good luck they howled to all on board.

Those by the rail above were waving goodbyes to people below shouting goodbyes as well. Sarah remembered the bedtime stories her father read to her. She worried for a moment about the Forty Thieves of Ali-Baba from bedtime stories.

"Mom, would Ali-Baba come to Morocco too? Sarah asked her mother.

"Of course not, honey-pie. We'll have English soldiers from the Crown to protect us from any harm. Her mom reassured her to erase her fears.

Chapter Four
Bedtime Stories

But later Sarah remembered about the largest band of thieves ever of Ali-Baba and of course she felt a bit scared.
"Mom, they rode on the fastest Arabian horses, and many go to the streets of Damascus and Bagdad, they ride down from the mountains, dad read that for me Sarah said still worried." Sarah honey-pie, listen to me now. These are stories only to make books fun to read. They are fun and bedtime tales only. You have nothing to fear. Her mother said looking sweetly into her eyes. "Are we going to travel by night mom? Peter says there are wolves in the deserts at night and they may be around too; is it true?

"Nonsense at all Sarah, dear. Do not worry anymore. We'll travel only when at day time. Think instead of dolphins we might see in the ocean. Think of whales we'll see jumping from the sea," her mother said, helping Sarah forget the Ali Baba thieves in her head.

"I'll get to ride on a camel! I'm sure my father will let me do it. I'm almost a grown-up man. He won't mind me doing that mom! "Peter said cheerfully and hoped a yes would come from his mother too.

"Nonsense, Peter, nonsense at all. I won't give you permission! Only the people from the desert travel by camels for they know how his mother said firmly.

"Are there wolves in the desert, like Peter says, mom? Sarah asked again to clear her mind of any worries.

"There won't be any in the desert, honey, and your brother knows that too; don't let Peter scare you, okay? Her mom said with her eyes on Peter's eyes to stop him from teasing his sister.

"C'mon Sarah lets go...we don't have much time! Before we know it will be the night! Come along quickly, let's go! Peter shouted and Sarah forgot all about her worries. She left behind her thoughts about thieves or wolves and ran with Peter.

"It's time to explore the ship," Peter said to Sarah.

He could not wait to roam around; he wanted to run from here to there. He stopped by the rail and Sarah trailed behind him to say goodbye to the people below. The people stood with hands up saying goodbye to all the little down at the port.

"Let's find our cabin mom! Peter shouted and walk briskly to find it their mother's cabin and once inside, they counted bunkers. "One and two and three, two bunker beds here. One on top for me! Peter pointed excitedly. "And this one in the middle is for me," Sarah said and jumped in there.

"The one next to the floor it's for mom! They said. Peter jumped in a hurry to the highest bunker. Sarah went into the middle. They planned for her mom in the bunker closer to her. The loud hoot of the ship called for their first destination.

"The ship will do a mail pick up; the Captain will pick mail in France and then in Portugal and then Cairo will be our final destination," their mom explained the trip from England to Egypt and back.

Hours later, Plymouth port vanished as the Castle-One sailed away from the port. The sun, before in front of the ship, now shone over the ship and by then, the promenading deck looked busy with many passengers on board. Families and children went walking leisurely, enjoying the warming sun.

"It's time Sarah to see the deck above, let's go now, run," Peter called her.

"Oh...so much fun we're going to have Sarah! Peter said pulling his sister's hand and running with her. Peter and Sarah left her mother behind them, then, both came back laughing to say.

"Look there! See the boats hanging on the side.! Sarah called his brother out this time and they ran again to look at the smokestacks; they smoked heavy darkened puffs of smoke into the air.

Sarah came after his brother both got to count the puffs. The shorter pipe puffed white steam three times! Sarah shouted while Peter ran away to hide from her.

"Let's go below! Peter said, let's see the boilers. The steam pushes the ship on the waters. We'll see engines bigger than the biggest whales in the sea of Norway.

"C'mon, we have to see them now," Peter said running already.

"We're on our way to Egypt wow! Peter said aloud. "Let's count rivet heads, look here," he said, and they ran again.

They looked at the smoke rising from the stack into the blue sky and Peter looked up at the sun squinting his eyes at the sky. He let the sun rays fall on his face.

"I can't, it makes my freckles bigger," Sarah yelled and both laughed running to the rail again.

"Yes, we'll find the White Camel and ride on his back, I swear, "Peter said to Sarah.

"I'm scared, Peter. Camels bite when they get angry father says," Sarah went saying she wouldn't ride on any camel.

"Don't be scared, Sarah. Remember just got to be brave? Just be like Tinker-Bell! We'll see the White Talking Camel, the King of Camels like Mr. Bernard said!! "Peter shouted.

"But our mom won't let us ride on a camel! Sarah shouted back. "I am not afraid of camels!

"I'll look for the White Camel and ride all alone," Peter said to his sister promising and crossing his heart not to be afraid and ride with him too.

"I can be his knight and he will be the King of the camels, I'll keep my eyes open that's what Mr. Bernard," said he yelling and running.

"But sand will hurt your eyes if you never close them! You can't do that Peter! Sarah shouted too running behind.

"He means to look round for the White Talking Camel. It might be close to us. But we may not see it if we're scared. Promise me. Please, Sarah, don't ever, ever never say you are afraid of camels. The White Talking Camel could hear you and would never come to us," he reminded her sister.

"I promise on the name of the Queen and the Crown," Sarah shouted to show him how brave she too could be and ran behind catching with Peter.

"Ok, cross your heart then. Now let us go see the engines. Don't be afraid. I'll ask our mother to come with us too, "Peter said already walking to face his mom. Mrs. Carnerhill rested under the shade not far from them in her chair reading a book of Egypt.

"Mother we want to see the engines room below. Can you please take us there now? Mother, please ask the Captain to give us permission," Peter said his blue eyes staring at her mother's eyes. Their mother said no at first. Then, she agreed and smiled. They went to seek the Captain's post and request a visit to the engines room. The Captain had left the helm to this Second in command and they walked away.

Minutes later the Carnerhill family walked to the dining area. The Captain who had heard Mrs. Carnerhill's request came to them and said, "If your mother says yes, I will personally take you. And you too Sarah can see the steamers below.

"Your father is a dear friend of mine. I visit him in Egypt every time I go," The Captain said to Peter and Sarah.

Their eyes glowed with pride. When lunch was over, the Captain took both children by their hands. Walking away to see the boilers below they went.

A half-hour later, the Captain towing the Carnerhill children each, on one hand, came back to the deck. He delivered the kids to their mom and left to his post behind the helm. It was early afternoon. The Carnerhill family walked on the upper deck for some time again.

After dinner time the family went back to their cabin for the rest of the night. The children were tucked in bed. Then, their mother read tales of Egypt for them.

Outside a full moon followed the ship moving slowly. Its hulls cutting the dark ocean water into white foamy sprays. The children closed their eyes and their mom kissed them good night.

The next day, the children jumped from their bunker beds. They rubbed their sleepy eyes to see it all through the ship's portholes. After breakfast, they quickly went up to the deck. They explored with excitement every inch of it. They met other children aboard and played many games and together they ran from one end of the CastleOne to the other.

They explored the ship asking questions. Their mother a few feet away sat on a chair and smiled pleased with them. Noontime came soon. The Captain took the children to his post. Once there he let Peter and Sarah get hands-on his "helm". Peter's head filled with images as the new Captain of the biggest ship of England.

That night Peter dreamed to be the captain on a ship of the Crown of England. Peter held the Captain's helm and Sarah was his Second in command.

"Aye, Aye, Sir," she said and their ship sailed away to Egypt. To the pyramids of Pharaohs of Egypt! Peter ordered and went away.

Once in Egypt, they traveled on the back of the White Talking Camel while they deeply slept cuddled in their bunkers and dreaming and dreaming again.

Chapter Five
On the Castle One

When the sun rose on the third day, the Great Rock of Portugal showed up at the distance. By noontime, the children went to lunch with Captain Williansmore and delighted they listened to new stories from the captain. That afternoon, they went up the deck and played with friends. They walked around and ran exploring the Castle-One. Later at dinner time, the Captain went to tell the story of the church of Fatima built on the Rock of Portugal.

"The story goes like this he said his eyes on the children on his table, "it was the year 711 of our Lord. The king of Morocco decided to invade Spain for he had heard of streets paved with gold stones in Spain. The King of the Moors wanted the gold nuggets for his kingdom! So, he sent his ships and thousands of his Moorish troops. He wanted the gold nuggets sailors said paved the streets of the old, old kingdom of Spain not too far away from Morocco just across the stretch only miles away."

"Did the Moorish take the gold from Spain? Asked Peter with curiosity in his voice.

"Well, not exactly Peter. But hear me finishing the story, "the Captain asked.

"Moorish ships arrived at the Iberian channel, which is now Spain's Gibraltar stretch. Listen to this well, children, on the Great Rock of Portugal, stood a little girl. She herded a flock of sheep and she was only seven years old! She saw many ships on the sea and she thought that's strange for she didn't see the flags of ships from Portugal.

"Nor she did see the flags of ships from Spain. Her mind worked quickly for she was smart. Those are ships invading us!! She told herself

"Ahh, but she was brave too. I must run now and tell the king of Portugal about warships! I'm strong. I can run fast. I'm going now to tell our king," she said to herself and decided to run; then she walked for a day under the sun at a good pace. And then ran again one whole night under the light of the moon too. The next day she arrived in Lisbon the capital of Portugal.

"She went straight to the king's castle and brought the news of the Moorish ships. A captain and his troop left on a horse for the king of Portugal. They went to the rock. They saw the ships on their way to Portugal and Spain, upon returning and told the king of Portugal.

"Many ships are on the ocean, your Majesty. The girl from Fatima is telling us the truth. They look like Moorish warships sailing on the sea. The king sent news to Spain. Their horses trotted day and night. They arrived to tell the Kingdom of Spain of the coming Moorish warships.

"That same day the king in Spain and his men prepared for the Moorish's invasion. From that day on, the girl was named the Brave Girl from Fatima and as she grew older and older Angels came for her when she passed away like an old, old lady. The kings of Portugal and Spain built a church just for her. It's there, right on the Rock of Portugal for people to remember her always. The Brave Fatima's Girl is buried there!

"The Captain cleared his throat getting ready and looked at Peter and Sarah and said, "Now, children to answer your question, young lad. No. The Moors never found in Spain the gold nuggets sailors said paved the street. But let me explain.

"The sun in Spain was so bright and so hot then and its rays turned stones golden and yellow.

"For golden nuggets, the Moors invaded Spain and stay in there for a thousand years, they say. For many years they look for gold in vain. And it took the Moorish many years to conquer Spain. They lived in Spain, but the Moorish went home when the brave knight Don Rodrigo-Diaz-de-Vivar won the last battle against the Moors."

By then, the Castle One has gotten closer to Portugal and the Captain invited the children to go up to the deck and they did. "Ahh....what we're going see now is the Great Rock of Portugal. From there, on that rock, the little girl from Fatima ran day and night to save the Kingdom of Spain and Portugal," the Captain said.

Minutes later, the Great Rock of Portugal showed up at the distance. The rock looking out to the sea for Moorish ships came about.

"Ahh....there it is..! The Great Rock of Portugal where the little girl from Fatima ran and ran, day and night to save the Kingdom of Spain and Portugal..! Peter said looking at the rock getting bigger as they moved closer to the rock.

When the Great rock of Portugal came into sight rising from the ocean below, both Peter and Sarah stood wide-eyed.
The ocean waves below crashed against the rocky mountain with big splashes, white foamy waves sprayed up into the air. The sun rays painted the rock with golden yellows on top, and also purples, browns, and bluish colors all around.

"Wow,..! Peter said. I can see the little town of Fatima! Up there in the mountains Sarah…do you…see….it? "Peter yelled.

"Yeah, I can see the red roofs and little white houses too, "Sarah said.

"If we could only step one day in Portugal tomorrow, "Peter said sharing his wish with Sarah.
Suddenly, the shape of the church of the Rock of Fatima rose against the blue sky. Its only tower the church rose to the air. It looked like saying hello! Or saying goodbye, Sarah said.

Peter and Sarah waved and waved! By then, the air was turning from hot to cool. A soft breeze was blowing already. It was beyond midafternoon of the next day when the ship left the Great Rock of Portugal behind and the children waved goodbye to saying goodbye to the great rock of Fatima's girl.

Sometime later the sun had died over them and many stars blinked on the darkened sky. Dinner time came about, and it was time to hear more mariners' stories from Captain. Their mother took them with her to their cabin to freshen up. At once again they got ready to walk back to the dining room. The table was set and at the corner, the Captain waited for his guests. Peter fidgeted excited next to Sarah for they had a thousand questions for their Captain.

The Captain for sure knows of the White Camel, he shared with his sister. He was eager to hear from the Captain too about the camel. He was determined to look everywhere and find the White Camel, he said to Sarah. His thoughts came to an end as the Captain welcome all to his table. Speaking again he began telling his guests about the Oldest Kingdom all in Europe.

The Kingdom of Portugal he began; it was very, very old and its King had fought valiantly too against the Moorish invaders. The king was only twelve years old more than Peter when becoming a king.

"Imagine for one second," the Captain said, "a child, a brave child and young as Peter Carnerhill. He pointed with one hand to him and went on to say. "Imagine yourself on a white horse and wielding your sword to defend your family and your country."

Peter indeed imagined himself a captain bravely fighting the Moors. He saw himself on top of his beautiful horse. He was wearing a golden armor shining under the bright sun. On her throne, her sister Sarah, now Queen of England, sat calling his knights to defend the land! His imagination came to an end when the Captain's voice commanded his attention. Peter couldn't wait. He had a million questions to ask their Captain and his hand he pushed into the air.

"Captain Williamsmore, "Peter said a bit shy at first. But then remembering to be brave, and have courage, he spoke like a young prince. He spoke clearly for all to hear him. "Have you Captain Williams more ever heard about the White Talking Camel of the desert? It's a camel that walks and runs everywhere. From here to there and everywhere and nobody can see or hear him for only brave children can. That's what Mr. Bernard my friend in London says?

The Captain in his chair said. "Of course, all legends and war stories I have heard. But of course, dear Peter going many times to the desert have heard about the White Camel. I have heard that story too. Oh...a thousand times indeed!

"However, let me tell you, my dear Peter. Unless you are a child of the brave and kind heart could never find the White Talking Camel. The King of camels indeed! They say it travels from here and there. He travels through an ocean of yellow sands. His coat turns on any color. It matches the sands at day or night time.

"Dark at night maybe and nobody then can see it when it hides for it takes on any color or anything. All you brave children here in my table today and going to Egypt, think, look around. Even in the middle of a day, the White Camel may be near. Ah, but you cannot see. A thousand times I heard the story. I tell you of the White Camel. Captains before me also heard of this camel! Oh, I regret a child I can no longer be, and I would find the White Camel. Be brave like Richard the Lion Heart our King of England past and you shall see it!

The Captain said good night to his passengers and to rest all went. Outside the night had fallen over the Castle-One. The ship headed quietly over the waters towards Morocco. A large and perfectly blue moon shone its pale light over the waters. Its pale silver rays like tinsel spread over the ocean in all directions when the children fell asleep. By midnight the ship got near the Gibraltar passageway, went through the sea separating the Spaniards from the Moorish.

The Pillars of Hercules people call the strait at one time, but it stands there now like pillars of Spain. While the ship kept on going seeking route on to its final port in Cairo, both Peter and Sarah dreamed the White Camel one more time.

Chapter Six
The Pillars of Hercules

The Pillars of Hercules are about to be seen. Our ship will pass through the stretch of Gibraltar..!! The Captain announced to his passengers now gathered on deck; all had come to see the old Pillars of Hercules. They saw the distant passage between Spain and Morocco; a sea passage of only a few miles. "The distance between the two countries is about ten miles only to be exact. Spain has two cities surrounded by Moroccan land on Africa," the Captain said.

The Captain was standing behind his helm, speaking over a loud horn for the passengers to hear him well and he said again, "the legend of the Romans says that Hercules traveled to climb the mountain of Atlas. Instead, he climbed a great mountain connecting the Mediterranean with the Atlantic sea.

"Hercules didn't find a passage from one sea to the other. He used then his superhuman strength. He smashed through the mountain with one fist.

"The hard rock broke into thousands of thousands of pebbles. All sank into the oceans making the sands. The large hole his fist made up is the passage we see now. "We call it nowadays the Gibraltar passage or Pillars of Hercules. Below the passage is Africa," he told the passengers on deck.

"On one side they saw Spain. The land of kings Ferdinand and queen Isabela who sent Columbus to discover America".

Then, the ship went slowly towards Spain seeking the passage of Gibraltar. On the opposite side, Morocco is the grand Moorish kingdom that extended to Spain also for a thousand years," the Captain said. Peter stood near the rail for some time, his eyes fixed on the land on either side. He imagined for a second the Moorish ships. All ships on their way to invade Spain.

Then, he imagined the Spanish warriors on their horses and the two sides ready for their battle and on the grand rock of Gibraltar the little Fatima girl, a brave girl from Portugal and the ship moved slowly on the warm waters of the Mediterranean Ocean.

The Captain called the port of Nador in Morocco his next stop. They would anchor there just after dinner time. Their ship would stay on their waters that night and depart the next day. Dinner came and the Carnerhill family joined the Captain's table again. Peter had a thousand and one questions for the Captain.

Would the Moorish people be their friends? Would the children play English games? Would they travel on their camels? Peter wanted to hear it all now and got ready for dinner time. When dinner time came up, he put his hand in the air asking permission from the Captain to speak and he said, " Captain Williamsmore, would you be there all the time? My mother and I and my sister Sarah had never been around at the Moroccan land?

"Oh, but of course, do not fear Peter and Sarah, he said. Moroccans are our friends indeed. They will chant and dance welcoming us. In fact, they will celebrate late into the night. Our ship will arrive with goods for the people from the markets of England. There is nothing to fear. We're going to be amongst friends.

We all sleep aboard and tomorrow we depart again from the port of Nador. Our next port is after Morocco is going to be in Tunisia. Then our destination port of Alexandria, in Egypt," the Captain said. Peter turned to his sister Sarah and whispered.

"We're going to hear their music and see magicians in Tunisia's port..! Wow...he said looking at Sarah. He imagined children feeding their animals. He imagined flocks of lambs and roaming milking goats. What an adventure this is, he told himself. He went to bed, but not wanting to sleep, not wanting to close his eyes and miss the fun. The moon's light entered through the little oval window on his bedside. Peter daydreamed about Tunisia and Egypt and Africa being a general, and captain and pirate in each of his dreams.

Early in the morning they went to the deck again and saw Moroccan land. The sun was softly warm when Peter heard the distant chants. The voice filled the air and his ears as well. He turned to his mom and asked about the man chanting.

"He is a faithful of God calling all to morning praying. Our churches have their bells to call to praying, here a man remind others to pray too," his mother explained.

"Oh, I can't wait to see it all," Peer said to Sarah.

"Can't wait either and see father too, "she said.

Sometime later, they went down from the ship to the grounds of the port. They found themselves roaming around in the Moroccan market. Many passengers have walked down to enjoy the plates of freshly Moroccan fruits. Colorful tables served with coconuts and sweetened figs. Others with walnuts and rice packed in little finger-like treats.

Many sweets ready to eat and everything Peter had imagined in his mind was there and more. Mountains of spices, some red, some yellow, some green and some brown piled like volcanoes, Peter told for Sarah and they giggled.

"Wow...all this food. Nobody can eat so much," Sarah said.

There were silvery smelly fish and orange crabs of large legs moving. Red shrimp and mushy squid everywhere in baskets ready for everybody to take away.

Also, a flock of furry lambs stood in the middle of the street; some quiet, some fidgeting and wanting to flee the care of a man. At the distance, a tall tower rose into the air. A man with his arms up sang again. Peter's eyes went to the man for a moment, then, he explored large heads of turnips and the yellow lemons next to coconuts and mangoes too. He touched the wrinkled prunes and onions the size of large snowballs.

Then, a camel cry was heard all the market. Overburdened by the heavyweight on its back, a camel had fallen to the ground refusing to get up and carry its load. It looked old and tired, Peter noticed and then its owner pulled a rope tied to the camel's snout and shouted impatiently. He tried to get the animal to its feet, but the camel didn't get stand up.

The man beat the camel with is a wooden stick on the snout and then its rump. Behind the large camel, an agitated calf cried alarmingly. Peter and his family walked closer to the animal on the ground and stood near.

"Get up you dirty lazy camel! Get up now..! You old beast! Good for nothing you old camel..! I'll give you the stick one more time! Get up or I'll put you to the grill, you good for nothing! I'm going to make you, meat for the market! Get up you lazy camel!

The man shouted upset and whipped the camel with his stick again and again. The camel got the punishment on its rump; it cried aloud and also the baby camel behind its mom. Peter's heart ached to watch the man's cruelty. The man hit the camel again; this time on its snout very hard. Sarah protested hanging to her mother's hand. "Oh, mom! Why he's punishing the camel," Sarah said saddened. "You're bad, man! She yelled at the man a few feet from them. Peter behind her sister, grabbed a large onion and pitched it across the air. The onion landed on the man's nose and he fell to the ground. Then, the man got up to his feet and turned around irate.

He was looking for his attacker, his face angry, but Peter stood by her mother and sister. He had grabbed two more onions ready to pitch them against the cruel man.

"You coward..! Do not hit the camel..! Peter screamed at the man as he stood from the dirt. The man walked to Peter, the man holding a wood stick and ready to hit the child. But then, the Captain came from behind the man and he stopped the man by grabbing his hand and ordered to stop his attack.

"Here," the Captain said, "here some coins. These children didn't mean to hurt you but to stop you from punishing your old camel. Take two coins. Take one for your bleeding nose. The other if you stop hurting the animal and go, "the Captain said firmly to the man.

The man returned to his camel and pulled the large camel from the rope around its snout. The animal stood under the heavyweight of its back and walked tiredly. Then, the man dragged the animal and left. Walking behind the large camel was a small baby camel. It went out running behind its mother as the man and his camels disappeared into the market. The people standing moved still gazing at Peter. The Captain stood with his mother and Sarah.

"You're brave. The two of you were and kind too. I'm proud to be your Captain. Please take a coin for the onion thrown to that man, "the Captain said to the merchant owner of the onions.

"No thanks. Here is a fresh juicy orange; one for the boy of brave spirit. Here, one for his kindness and one for her kindness too."

The merchant said smiling at Peter and Sarah giving them oranges. Minutes later, the Captain and his passengers entered a hostel just near and rested there from the sun. They ordered lemonades and waited under the shade of the canopy above them.

"You've done what others might have not done. You defended the camel from an unkind man. Camels are diligent and strong, but also get tired when very old.

Now," the Captain said, "you are free to visit the market for two hours." 'We're going to depart again for Tunisia. Tomorrow we're going to be in Alexandria port of Egypt."

An hour or so later, Captain called all passengers aboard the Castle One. Peter and Sarah climbed up the ramp to the ship. They both wanted to be number one on the deck and minutes later they were aboard again.

The next port of Tunisia was in Peter's head when they stood by the rail to say goodbye to the Moroccan children below.

"Goodbye, goodbye, "both Peter and Sarah said pushing their hands up in the air.

"Goodbye, goodbye.! many children yelled smiling. All running as the ship moved away. The Tunisian port one day away then comes Alexandria," Peter said excitedly to Sarah and both smiled.

Chapter Seven
The Thieves

The ship had stayed in Morocco half a day when the Captain announced the next port would be in old Tunisia. It was night when the Castle-One drop anchor at the port. The next day Peter and Sarah ran to the rail wanting to see the Tunisian port city. The story said it was part of the Atlas mountain range of the Sahara desert. The Tunisian country at thousand years old country was very old, their mother said. It was part of the Atlas' mountains. Their mother told them about Hannibal the Tunisian; a great military commander considered by many one of the best in history, their mother explained.

"Was he better commander than Alexander the Great mother? Peter asked.

"It's hard to say. But the two men are considered great Generals," her mother said.

"Did his men ride on warring elephants for real from Spain to invade Italy mother as father read? Peter asked.

"Yes, they trained the elephants and men rode on them Peter, " his mom said.

"The brave Hannibal marched with hundreds of warring elephants from Spain to Rome! He took over Italy for over fifteen years son," their mother said. Peter imagined himself riding on the back of a warring elephant and himself commanding thousands of men from Spain to Rome, like a great general.

"Sarah, just imagine for a moment! You and me riding on the back of a huge elephant. Elephants can take us anywhere we want to go. We would then go through mountains and rivers, wow! We could go anywhere! Peter told his sister.

"I would be scared. The elephant could get me with his trunk, "Sarah said. "Be brave, remember? Peter said and ran to the deck.

"Let's go back and look around before we sit for lunch, " he asked Sarah.

The two children ran to the deck. Their mother followed them as they walk everywhere and both children stopped here and there. Other times they went to discover anything while they also stopped and talked to other children. Peter and Sarah went on to the deck along with their mother. They walked and ran. They made friends again and soon the moon rose over and evening came again. It was time to rest have dinner and get to bed. Once in bed, their mother read about the Seven Wonders. Alexandria was one of the Seven Wonders in the old world. She said reading slowly for them. Peter asked his mom what are the other Wonders?

"I'll tell you quickly for is getting late," she said looking at the children getting sleepy eyes already.

"Well, let me see if I remember them all. The Seven Wonders of the Ancient World were the Great Pyramid of Giza we're going to see soon. The Hanging Gardens of Babylon, they don't exist anymore. Also, the Temple of Diana where she was the goddess of the hunt and the moon. She talked to all the animals the story goes.

"Also, the Statue of Zeus at Olympia who was a giant seated figure of Zeus, the head of all Gods of the Greek people in the old days. The statue of Zeus was over forty feet tall. It was from the water to the deck of this ship! She said and listened to these children quietly. The statue was made by a Greek important sculptor named Phidias.

He made it more than twenty-five hundreds of years ago! People went to see his ivory and gold plates in the Temple of Zeus.

"What's a sculptor mom? Sarah asked.

"Well, let's see here. A sculptor is like someone who draws and paints. Instead of drawing and painting on paper.

"He draws the face or the whole body on someone on a piece of stone; or instead of painting with brushes, he uses tools called chisels, some large, some small but very sharp. Then, with chisels, a sculptor cuts into the stone.

'He cuts out the lips and the ears and the eyes and the hands until one can see what the sculptor wanted to cut out from the stone, " her mother explained and went on saying. Now, also, the one wonder was the Colossus of Rhodes also called the Lighthouse of Alexandria; you Peter know already what it is. All others will be our story for another day," their mother said.

"What's a Wonder? Sarah asked cuddling closer to her mom.

"A Wonder is something very unique and very special as you and you! Alexandria was the most important city in the Mediterranean sea at one time. Its lighthouse was the largest ever built in the old days. Ship captains could see in the darkest of nights Alexandria's lighthouse from afar. They could see it from hundreds of miles, even in the worst of storms," their mother said.

Both children listened with great curiosity, but their eyes were slowly closing with heavy sleep.

"The city, their mother said again, is very old. More than a thousand years old.

"The great Alexander of Greece ordered it to be built. Yes, he wanted all sailors to be guided by its lighthouse when lost at sea, "she whispered for them and went on.

"Alexander built it to be the largest. It had more books than any other library in the world in those days. Ah, but that is not all.

"The city had also a queen named Cleopatra. Marc Anthony a Roman general presented the queen with a gift. Over two hundred thousand books he sent her! Their mom said.

"Two hundred thousand books...wow! They would sink the largest ship in England. Peter said and they laughed.

"So, tomorrow morning, their mother said, "we're going to see the port of Tunisia. A day after we're going to see the great city of Alexandria. A city built more than a thousand years ago! More than a thousand years ago and that's before England or France, think children! She said that to wake up the children's imagination.

"I'll dream about the lighthouse of Alexandria! Its light signaling the Castle One as the ship moves closer and closer to the port, "Peter said.

"I would like a dream of me on top of a baby-elephant. It would be very small, a baby elephant with large trunks. It would protect me from any of Ali-Baba's thieves, "Sarah said softly half-sleep.

The next, daylight entered early through the little portholes windows of the ship and Peter's eyes gazed at the port of Tunisia. At first, it looked tiny then, it grew and grew and grew larger. Finally, it got bigger as the ship got very close to the shore. The ship hooted aloud and let people on board know they had arrived at the port of Tunisia. By midmorning, the ship entered the Tunisian port and it dropped anchor to stay fixed on the water. Then, one by one all passengers walked down the ship's ramp.

Peter and Sarah dragged their mom as they hurriedly walked to the port's grounds. They followed the Captain to the visitors' house and Peter and Sarah begged their mom to take them to explore the market. They wanted to see the market firsthand.

"Let's look for a baby camel I can pet," Sarah said without fear.
"Children you cannot touch! The merchant may demand that we buy it. Keep your hands off any items we don't need to buy," their mother explained.

"But mom, there are millions of things to see and touch. Also animals to pet and get close to pet," Peter complained.

"Be careful their mother warned. You cannot touch any animals. Some may bite your hand. Do not feed them or get to close. Do not touch any fruits and food, fresh fish and especially goats either they will chew on your fingers. Please do not touch anything or up to the ship we go, right? Their mother warned but everything invited the children to look around and they walked from one place to the next followed by their mom nearby.

The merchants offered their goods and pointed to them while the children stopped and only looked obeying their mom. Sometimes laughing and running from here to there. Their mother kept walking faster behind them as they walked from shop to shop.

"Mom, I'm not scared of camels more," Sarah said.

"I know you're not afraid any more honey-pie," her mom said catching with her.

"I want to be brave like the girl from Fatima! Sarah said looking at her mom.

Her mom smiled at her softly and saying yes dear. The children's eyes glowed with delight at the sight of the market as they walked through the people. Merchants and visitors all there at the same time. Peter's eyes caught the gleaming of rows of pots; some made of bronze and some of the brass. They hang everywhere from merchant's tents and all glittered with light; gleaming with every waft of breeze pushing them around even more. Then came to sight multicolored hand-woven carpets.

"Imagine you and me flying on a flying carpet," Peter said to Sarah. She giggled looking back to carpets all over on the ground of the open market.

"I would fly very low. I won't scrape if I fall, "Sarah said.

"I would go very high and see it all from above," Peter said with sparkles in his eyes.

Suddenly, everything thundered! The heavy pounding of horses' hooves shook the ground. Women screamed in panic and tried to hide with children while merchants lowered their tents and covered their goods! People screamed everywhere! The howling of many men filled the air in the market! "Thieves are coming!

Thieves...thieves....are coming to rob us!!

Chapter Eight
Taken to the Desert

The merchants shouted their warnings and women wailed and hid their children away. The desert thieves rode in their horse to rob them. A dozen thieves dropped to the ground dismounting from their horses. They had swords in hand and moved from store to store; some threatened and pushed merchants and shouted at them demanding their money. Peter hid behind a large bag of spices.

His mother and Sarah hid a few feet from him; both squatted down behind big sacs of cinnamon and figs.

The two stayed down and quiet while a thief robbed the merchant of the shop. Then, the thief walked around the shop looking for fruit or else to take with him. Suddenly, Sarah hiding behind her mother screamed. The little monkey above them grabbed her hair and scared her. Alerted by her scream, the man looked and listened. Then, he walked suspecting a mother hiding a child from him. He walked back to where Sarah had screamed and found her and her mother hiding from the thief.

"Hahaha," the man laughed and said something in his own language.

Both mother and daughter froze in fear, but they stood unmoving and brave. The man walked closer to them. He looked at Sarah's red hair and smiled reaching for it and touching it. He held Sarah's hair in his hand and a grin came to his face.

Then, he said something in his foreign language just for himself again. Sarah's mom protested and slapped the thief's hand.

He laughed and then pushed Sarah's mother to the ground. The thief then grabbed Sarah from her waist. Peter came out from hiding.

Peter ran bravely ramming his head into the man's waist and wrestled with the man. The thief grabbed Peter by an arm and laughed aloud. He gazed at him and dragged Peter with him too. With both children at his hands, he left seeking his horse. It took the band of thieves only a few minutes to rob the merchants of the market. Then, they jumped onto their horses and left with anything they wanted to have.

Peter squirmed kicking the man's legs while Sarah screamed for help. Her mother stood up from the ground to get her children back and ran outside after them! But all seemed too late. The thief was on his horse trotting away. Peter was pushed down on his stomach as he tried to dismount from the horse.

The thief tied him down quickly to the horse's saddle as the thief's horse went out of the market with the English children on his mount. Sarah kicked and bit the man. She was unafraid of him, but he tied her down too. Peter and Sarah were taken on the horse's mount to the desert.

Hours later in the desert, when the heat of the sun fell on the caravan, a man came to Peter and Sarah to look at them and wrapped them in desert linens to protect them from the sun. Then, the group of camels went on West under the heat of the sun above that scorched them as they traveled. Peter's eyes gazed around seeking a route to escape, but the desert looked the same in every direction. Sarah's face had turned from pinkish and freckled to a tomato red. That afternoon the caravan drove the camel and horses to an Oasis and the desert thieves set up an encampment there. A bonfire in the middle of it kept them warm through the cold night.

Once on the sands, Peter told his sister that soon they would be going home and not to worry. He thought about a Genie's lamp. It could be anywhere in the desert. If they could find it, they would be saved in the blink of an eye.

Just one wish from its Genie and they would be home, he said. It would grant them three wishes and they would go home, he imagined himself with the magic lamp under his arm. A Genie popping at once perhaps will get us to see the treasure-filled mountains of Ali-Baba too! He said trying to cheer up his sister sobbing and sad.

"Who knows if we get to see the gold! And see treasures that filled their trunks, "he told his sister Sarah to stop her crying and make her happy again. He imagined the enormous stone and the gate opening to his command. Inside the cave all the treasures of Ali-Baba and his forty thieves," he told Sarah and she stopped crying.

When Sara went to sleep and she could not hear him anymore, Peter laid next to her. He felt like crying too for a second or two but wanted to be brave indeed. The story of the White Talking Camel entered his head. Mr. Bernard's story returned to his mind. He closed his eyes wanting to sleep too.

The thieves sat around the fire keeping an eye on their camels and the children around. He heard their guffaws celebrating; their voices sounded loud in the silence of the night. Peter put his face down on the coarse pellet, but after a while, he fixed his eyes on the small twisters of sands. Every now and then, tiny grains of sand danced pushed by the wind.

They flew in the air and up they went away like tiny stars as they gleamed in the breeze going up and up flying away. His eyes traced them wishing to fly like them. They flew like sparks of glittering gold. Up and up they went as Peter glared at them imagining flying with them away and away. He gazed at the sky and he closed his eyes.
Somehow he knew they would be saved.

"Be brave Peter like a knight! He reminded himself. Then, he thought again about the White Talking Camel and asked him to help them! Yes, help us escape, he said to himself and closed his eyes too.

Unbeknown to Peter and Sarah, the White Talking Camel had come already; he was looking after them. The next day, the caravan got ready again and went South through Tunisia and Peter could understand the children's language and anything the thieves said to each other. By midday, they stopped outside a tiny village and the men watered their camels. The pouch with camel's milk went from child to child. Peter and Sarah took some of it, for now, they knew it would be a long, long trip. Sarah asked Peter where the men were taking them. They're headed to Libya, a country South and far from Tunisia, Peter thought.

Tal-Mishem, the Talking Camel, had answered their questions right in Peter's heads without him noticing yet. Tunisia, Peter said to himself and then to Sarah, "it is the country of Barbarossa the red beard pirate Sarah! That's what dad read to us one day remember?

Peter said. We've traveled from the port of Tunis and we're now going South, but don't worry for mom and dad are coming for us," Peter said.

"Tunisia is the smallest of the countries in Africa. We're going to travel for a few days only. We're going to travel through the Atlas mountain of Hercules, and we may even see the city of Carthage. The city of Hannibal and warring elephants, remember? Sarah reminded her brother as if she had all that in her head too.

"Do you see that tower? Peter asked.

"Yes, it looks like a tall castle in England, "Sarah said.

"That's their place for praying. They call it the Great Mosque of Kairouan and it's the oldest in the world! Wow, it's the oldest, about a thousand years old, Sarah," Peter said.

"I see no trees of fruits here, Peter. Do they eat fruits like in Morocco?

"Well, at one time these gardens and orchards were here too and there were water canals and everything was green, Dad told me that," Peter remembered. "Pirates robbed ships going by from Greece to Italy or Spain and those coming here. They also cut their trees and sold their woods," Peter said.

"Are the pirates still at sea? Sarah asked fearfully.

"No, of course, no, Sarah. It was a long time ago when they lived, "Peter said proudly remembering his father's stories.

"Why do the people say "Bon Jour in the morning and Adieu for goodbye? Sarah asked.

"After the Turkish people lived here also the French people live here for many years and people learned French too " Peter explained.

"Do they know English too?

"I think so Sarah, but some also talk in Italian," Peter said.

Sometime after the great lake of Tunis came to sight and the caravan and its camels and children prepared to stop at the lake and spend the night there. They traveled many days and many nights from the port of Tunis. The caravan with the children had left behind the old city of Sfax.

Chapter Nine
The Talking Camel

As the caravan moved again through the desert that afternoon, a dusty "sandstorm" was coming their way and winds grew stronger blowing sand and whistling over their heads. The thieves, the children, covered their heads while the camels knelt to the ground. The camels made a circle around everybody to protect them from the sands storm and the wind. The camels stayed with their bellies to the ground; their eyes protected by thick eyelashes and protected by their rough, thick furry coats. The animals protected all from the storm. Mountains of sand flew over them like a sea typhoon of sand going over their heads while wind whined and hissed through the desert for some time.

Peter and Sarah cuddled together and next to them a large camel knelt on the sand. A camel's pelt covered their heads and after a while, the sandstorm passed, and the hot sun came out again hotter than ever. The camels were pulled up by the reins and stood ready to go. Peter forgot all about the camel story for some time and Sarah smiled again without fear.

Sometime after, the caravan traveled without stopping to rest and a few hours later they entered a village just when the sun was hiding behind the roofs of the village's houses. It looked like a yellow egg yolk floating in the air.

Peter looked around and saw a fowl of sheep and goats roaming freely. Close to the animals, a boy wrapped in white linens herded them around all by himself. He waved to the children and all waved back their goodbyes. Once in the village, a man let the camels stop at his water hole marked by a ring of stones and few palm trees. The camels were given water again and the trees offered them shade and a place to rest. When all the camels quenched their thirst, water pouches were filled and water was given to children.

When darkness fell over them and sprinkling stars covered the sky, it was time to seek a place to sleep and pass the night. Peter and Sarah sat among the other children who had gathered by the fire. The men and children sat facing each other while the camels knelt a few feet behind.

Two of the oldest children were ordered to pick the camels' dung to keep the fire for the night. Peter and Sarah sat to play and to count the tiny ashes rising up like fireflies into the sky with every breeze of air. Soon, the other children in their caravan imitated their game and they moved closer to talk. They asked their names and how old they were. They asked each other about their brothers and sisters and said they could always be friends.

They promised to do that then and play their games together. So, they counted the sparks going up the air also. They laughed and giggled having fun being friends. They forgot for some time about bad times making new friends. Then, they told each other tales and stories.

Some were spooky and some not too scary, but some about the bogeyman. Sarah told them about Santa Clause on Christmas day. How he went up the roof and down the chimney. The children laughed hearing he was big and round but climbed the roof of houses in every town. She told them how he carried a sac with free toys for all children in the world. The children wondered how he went around visiting so many towns in so many countries with toys for all children in town.

Then, Sarah told them about the Red Nose Reindeer named Rudolph and its team of flying deer that took Santa flying everywhere.

The children asked Sarah when he was coming to their land and give them toys. She told them of days children played to be ghosts in Halloween. She told them about trick or treat candies children were given and they wondered why. She told them about the Queen of England! She told them about the Crown and its many ships on the oceans while the children listened in silence. They had never heard of India or China, nor they had ever heard of Honk Kong and America for they didn't have books. All countries were so far from the deserts, they said wide eye opened.

And Peter and Sarah listened too for the children knew many stories and shared with them. The children told stories in their own language, but Sarah and Peter understood well for The Talking Camel sitting near them talking quietly translated for them; he helped them understand each other and be happy as new friends. So, the children told Sarah about Tut the boy and king, the youngest Pharaoh of Egypt.

They told her about the animals in Africa and many then never had heard of before. They talked about the white rhinoceros of many trunks on its snout. They told her of hippos as large as the Castle One ship. They told her about giraffes as tall as coconut trees. And of course, about the old mines of gold, rubies, and diamonds of king's Solomon down in the heart of Africa. Then, about the stories of the black Queen of Sheba from the African jungles and much, much more to remember forever and ever.

When the game came to its end, Peter and Sarah went to lay next to each other. The men sat around the fire and the children went down to sleep again. All camels rested on their bellies not too far from Peter and Sarah. The camels sleeping cuddled next to each other and Peter turned his head to look at the animals. A few feet from him a camel snorted aloud, and Peter noticed. He looked at the camel, and the camel looked straight at him with its brown walnut size, honey brown eyes on his snout. His coat looked brighter than all others, Peter thought. Its fur smooth and soft, with a white blinking glow.

His eyes of large and thick eyes lashes seemed to stare at him, he thought again. Suddenly, as he gazed again at the camel, the camel flared its nostrils and wiggled its nose winking an eye at Peter. Peter already half-sleep but surprised winked an eye at the camel too. Amazed Peter look again just as the camel showed his white teeth in a large grin winking at him one more time. Peter sat wanting to wake up Sarah but the camel stared t him and winked an eye one more time and he heard in his mind, "Hello Peter, is me, the Talking Camel, don't be afraid." To Peter's surprise, the camel winked back and smiled a grin of white teeth.

Peter winked twice rapidly in a game of eye winking winks and giggled. The camel imitated him with two rapid winks. Peter giggled and the camel showed his white teeth as if pleased with their game of winks. Then Peter winked three times slowly. The camel did exactly the same winking his eyes slowly too. Then, Peter winked fast four times counting. The camel winked four times too as fast a Peter Then, suddenly Mr. Bernard's words came to Peter's mind. He remembered them exactly like this.

"He may even wink at you if he wants to talk to you". Peter remembered and of course, he knew it! It was the White Talking Camel!! He turned to his sister, but Sarah sleeping already but startled he stayed still on the pelt next to his sister. Then he closed his sleepy eyes and put his head to the sand. It's my imagination, he thought but before he could close his eyes, a puff of air ruffled his hair! The camel only a few feet before him spoke again. He was tall and strong.
His body seemed covered with a gleaming coat almost snow white. Peter freaked out. His heartbeat faster in his chest. Then, he saw the camel's lips moving; talking just in the way humans talked, he noticed. Then, the camel moved closer to Peter, and his words got into Peter's head.

"Wow!! Peter said aloud.

"Listen up Peter, it's only me the camel," said the voice friendly. Remember me, the White Talking Camel Mr. Bernard told you about? I'm real, indeed, the camel said and snorted on him a puff of air. Peter could not believe it. He called out his name so clearly; he felt frozen for a second. But then, the White Talking camel called his name clearly one more time.

The camel sounded just like Mr. Bernard the mail clerk, he told himself. The sound went straight into his head as the camel called his name three more times. Peter's eyes felt heavy as never before and just wanted to sleep but before he did just that closing his eyes, Peter heard the camel again. His soft voice words wishing him good night. "Good night Tal-Mishem, Peter said not knowing why before closing his eyes while falling already into a dream.

The next morning, as soon as Peter opened his eyes, he stood up, and he looked to where the camel was the night before.

"Sarah!! He said filled with happiness, "that's the camel; that winked and talked to me last night! It winked an eye and he spoke to me Sarah, believe me, he did!!

"Go talk to him, Peter! Sarah looked at him and said as happy Peter but before that Peter looked in the direction of the camel; it stood to chew something. His snout was long and his eyes walnut brown.

"He's tall and looks strong, but his coat is just like that of any other, Peter thought. "That one there, it's the camel I'm sure," Peter yelled winking an eye at the camel.

The camel brown eyes looked at him for a second but never winked at him or never grinned like the night before.

"It may not be the same, or maybe it was just a dream," Peter said disappointed.

"Do you think that he would talk to me, Peter? Sarah asked, without doubt, he was indeed the camel from Mr. Bernards' fairytale.

"Don't know……it doesn't even want to wink at me now Sarah. Don't know why! Peter said.

"Wink at him harder now, like this, do like this, hard, for some time," she asked Peter for Sarah never doubted her brother's words. But Peter just sat on the sand sad this time for the camel never winked at him that morning. Peter tried a couple times more before giving up and turning to Sarah also sad.

"Maybe he only winks at night," said Sarah.

"Maybe, you right Sarah," Peter said and looked away.

"I'll show you tonight if you stay awake, he may come again," Peter promised. It was time to keep traveling and a man came to put them on a camel. "I cross my heart, I try to stay awake too," Sarah promised as she sat up to watch the camel's eyes and see if he would blink at her too.

Chapter 10
New Destination

Later that morning, the caravan left the site for a new destination. Peter perched in front of the camel's hump held the reins while Sarah held to his brother and covered her face from the scorching sun. Peter could not wait for the sun to go down and night to come again. Was it just a dream? Peter asked himself thinking while on the camel. Why wasn't the camel speaking to him now? Why? If he said that he came to help us. He asked. Finally, the day came to its end several hours later. A fire was set up and thieves and children sat around it. Everybody slept when Peter laid down facing the camel.

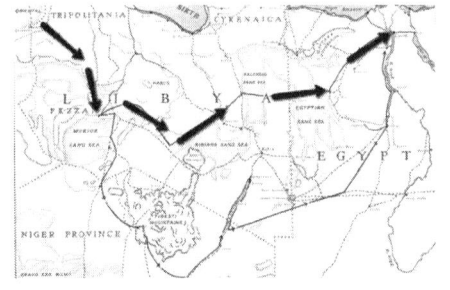

He spoke to Sarah hoping to keep her awake. He waited for the camel to wink or speak to him again, but the camel never winked or talked to him. His coat never glowed either. He was about to close his eyes when he heard the words in his mind.

"Peter it's me. I am sorry Peter. Sorry indeed. But I cannot speak or wink at you while the others are awake. Not even in front of little Sarah. She's too young and I might even scare her too, "Tal-Mishem said in Peter's mind.

Peter understood every word the camel said mentally for this time he didn't move his lips as humans do. The words had never come out of the camel's mouth, he thought. Then, the animal's lips moved up and down with each word again. All words pronounced in clear English. Peter remained mute without saying a word as if he had seen a ghost of some sort.

"Peter, Peter, you're okay? The camel puffed a warm ball of air at Peter's face. "Uhh, your breath stinks," Peter complained clipping his nose. "Yeah…I think so, but it will pass, don't worry," the camel said and laughed saying again, I am Tal-Mishem you know, but some call me TM. I like it too for children like Sarah can't remember or say my name," the camel said with a grin showing its teeth.

"Can I call you TM then? Peter said.

"Oh, please just call me TM, that's fine! Tal-Mishem replied.

"That's fine for me too, Mr.TM," Peter said and giggled.

"And please don't shout whenever you talk to me. Your words get in my head too loud. "Just think about what you want to tell me. I'm going to understand your thoughts, every word in them, Peter," the camel whispered mentally.

"I am dreaming again perhaps," Peter said to himself and closed his eyes.

"Peter look around you. Pinch your cheeks," Tal-Mishem said and Peter did.

"Ouch, it hurts, " he said.

"Of course." The White Talking Camel laughed. For a second he sounded like Mr. Bernard, Peter thought.

"Peter, I am Tal-Mishem the White Talking Camel indeed. The Talking Camel, remember me? I'm here to help you and your sister to escape. To help you go home, " Tal-Mishem said.

The camel's words got into Peter's mind clearly. Peter thought of awakening Sarah again. His eyes grew the size of geese eggs very white and round. Only a tiny speck of blue-stained the whiteness of his eyeballs.

He wanted to say something, but his tongue got stuck as if frozen indeed. He could not move it to say a word. When his tongue loosened up, he called out his sister's name.

"He is talking to me indeed Sarah, Sarah wake up now! Peter said almost yelling.

When he turned his head around, the camel was gone. It had gone to be with the herd of camels knelt now on the sands. They all rested just a few feet from the children. Some chewed with sleepy eyes; some cuddle next to each other while others with half-closed eyes rested on their bellies. None looked like they could talk or glow.

They all look alike," Peter told himself and went down to sleep again next to Sarah.

That night, Peter dreamed of the White Talking Camel like many times before. He rode on his back and together went through the desert. They came across the pyramids of Giza that looked like a gigantic golden triangle from the air. The next morning, Peter couldn't tell what was real and what was not from his dreams the night before. I dreamed of this camel, he repeated. One side of him wanted to tell his sister Sarah. The other side of him said no I cannot tell her now.

He decided to keep it a secret and do like the camel had asked to do.

"Did the camel blink its eye to you last night Peter?"

"I will tell you later," Peter said as s man with the milk pouch came to the children; he put the pouch in front for them to drink the sour camel's milk.

"Drink as much as you two can. We won't stop until this evening if you puke it, I'll have you eat sand the whole day," the man said picking up the heavy leather pouch.

Then he poured the greasy milk into the kids' open mouths. Peter understood every word the man said.

"Don't worry Peter. I've made your mind understand his language," Tal-Mishem said staring at Peter.

Like round walnut and brown eyes from the distance, he thought. Minutes later, a man came and dragged the children to where a camel stood. The camel driver hit the camel with a stick on the animal's chins.

The camel went down on his knees for the children to climb up to its loins. The camel pushed first its rump, then its front legs until it stood again full height. Peter and Sarah sat on the camel's back. Peter took the reins and held to them hoping not to fall. Slowly, with heavy steps, the camel walked the single lane of camels and followed them walking into the desert again. The caravan of thieves and children went into the desert as the sun rays were beginning to warm up. Sometime later, desert heat became hot, very hot making the children thirsty and sweaty.

About midafternoon, a small village of sun brick houses appeared in the distance where the houses looked reddish under the heat of the desert; all pushed against each other like a giant beehive with doors and windows, "Pete told Sarah and they giggled.

They got closer to the houses and a pack of skinny, slinky dogs came out barking at the camels. The caravan passed by the outside walls of the town and sometime later, they stopped by a well far behind the village. That evening, when the sun left and the sky was without light and dark, the men set up the fire again. One of them brought a stick with meat to Peter and Sarah for dinner and he went away. They began roasting morsels of meat on sticks and after their meal, they ordered all the children to feed the camels.

"When came to one, he heard clearly, "Listen, Peter, and pay attention because soon we're going escape. We've traveled for many days now since we left the port of Tunis behind. We went through the city of Sfax and lakes Itchkeul and Red lake."

"And we're going to come across deserts surrounding," TalMishem said.

"It's just a desert everywhere, so much desert," Peter said,

"Oh, yes, but tens of thousands of years ago, the Sahara Desert was very green with vegetation everywhere.

"It had many lakes, forests, and animals. It had so much life every where," Tal-Mishem said as if remembering being there in the past.

"What happened to water and trees Tal-Mishem? Peter asked.

"Aah, that's a long story, Peter and we're going to talk about that in the future. Let me tell you about the people here. They have lived here for over five thousand years. Even before the Phoenicians and the Greeks came here to sell their goods to people in here when it was known as Tripoli, which meant three-cities," Tal-Mishem explained to Peter.

"Was Tripoli bigger than London?

"Indeed, Peter, it was called Tripoli which means three-cities in one as I said. The Phoenicians settled here, then the Greeks and then the Romans. Later, also the Turkish and they all fought for Libya, " TalMishem said.

"Are we going to stop by the lake? Peter asked.

"Yes, our camels are tired and thirsty and it's a beautiful place to rest, "Tal-Mishem said.

"Have you been to the lake? Peter asked.

"Oh, yes, many times and many lakes Peter. Like lake Itchkeoul, Red lake and the Great lake of Tunis.

"They're all beautiful places to be around, Tal-Mishem told Peter and went on to say. "Tomorrow we're going to enter the city of Burayqah when we go across to its other side, we're going to be ready. We're going to escape from there and cross the desert and keep traveling until we're in Egypt." Tal-Mishem sent the message to Peter's head.

"Are we going to travel through the desert again in one day?
"Not exactly one day, Peter. Our last journey before we get to Egypt is going to be through the Libyan desert next to Egypt.
"It will take us many days unless we could fly. We need to prepare for our trip, "Tal-Mishem explained.

"Can you really fly TM," asked Peter remembering Mr. Bernard's story.

"Well, that's very tricky sometimes, Peter. We'll see when the time comes," Tal-Mishem said and winked at an eye at Peter.

Chapter Eleven
The Escape Plan

Peter had just awakened to the new morning as if he had just closed his eyes. His eyes felt heavy with sleep and the images of the camel winking at him during the night remained in his head. He ran his eyes from camel to camel. None look like the camel that winked at him, he thought. There was no white camel of a glowing coat. He stood up and walked to the site where the camel had stood the night before and simply puffed in the air. This was the second night he dreamed of the camel, he told himself. The sands looked smooth. It was a dream, after all, he thought.

"Sarah wake up, Sarah get up now," he said to his sister.

The man with the pouch of milk came to them again. He signaled for him to open his mouth. Peter doubted for a second. The eyes of the man looked at Peter hard and he did open his mouth. The man brought the pouch to Peter's mouth and squirted some. The greasy camel's milk filled his mouth. It didn't taste as bad, he thought. When Peter finished, the man signaled to Sarah. Peter guessed quickly.

"He wants you to drink some of the milk, "Peter said to Sarah his sister.

"Don't want any, it stinks," Sarah complained covering her mouth with a hand refusing to open her mouth, but the man pressed his dark fingers around Sarah's mouth. Her lips made a circle, a fish's mouth and the man squirted twice in her rounded lips the camel's milk.
Sarah swallowed hard. The man laughed aloud and left.

The man threw the milk pouch on Peter and told him to drink too. You're too skinny, you won't get a purse any gold," he said and walked away.

"Open your mouth Sarah; it will help you feel better, "Peter said lifting the pouch for her have some of it again.

"Allah, we must get his weight in gold, or we'll leave him behind with the skinny ones," a man by the fire shouted as they saw Sarah's drinking from the pouch. The men all laughed again looking at them.

Soon, all horses and camels stood ready for its riders. A man picked Sarah and dumped her on the hump of a camel. Then, he picked Peter and did the same, putting him in front of her. Peter grabbed the reins put on his hand and when did, the camel turned its long neck. Its large eyes stared at him and he winked a sleepy eye to Peter. Before anything, the camel's voice went into Peter's head. "Peter it's me, TalMishem. Yeah, yeah, I know there is no glow. I may look different, but trust me, it's me, TM," the camel said mentally and the words got into Peter's head and he grinned remembering all about the Talking Camel and Mr. Bernard back at London.

"May I tell Sarah we're riding on your back now? Peter asked.

"Not yet. Now, listen up. I have two round little stones in my ears; they are like what you children in England call...wait I can't find the English word for them. Anyway, we call one the Miru and the other the Nimut. But never mind their names.

"Marbles maybe," Peter said.

'Aah, yes, of course, foolish of me not to remember the names you call them; marbles, yes, marbles," TM said.

"Wow, Peter said thinking of those he used for playing Keepsies with his friends.

"They sort of magic marbles; they would make you giggle sometimes. Yeah, that's it. Now, these marbles are more than that. These are going to help you talk to me and Sara all at the same time.

When you hold them in your hand you can talk to me. Simply keep them together, " TM explained.

"Magic marbles wow! Peter said with surprise in his face.

"Now, Peter, you will find them in the sac on the mount on my back. Keep them close to you. Do not lose them for without them you can't call me or talk to me. Now put your hand in the pouch and grab the magic marbles. Put them in your pocket. Whatever you do Peter, make sure you have them with you. The green is for you, the red is Sarah's and the blue is mine; leave it in the sac."

"Now, please put the blue marble back in the sac. Do you understand? Tal-Mishem the talking camel asked.

Yes I do, "Peter said with his hand already inside the sac. A giggling feeling ran through his fingers. Peter pulled his hand still giggling.

"Sorry, I forgot.

"Don't be afraid. You'll get used to their tickling in your hands soon. The more you hold them the better and the more you will enjoy the feeling, "Tal-Mishem said and TM went to explain that if he was holding hands with Sarah she would hear him too and the three would hear each other.

"Wow! Peter said giggling.

"Tonight, we're going to rest outside the village. When everybody is sleeping, I will visit Sarah. I'm coming to Sarah in her dreams. I'll tell her about me and the giggling marbles. You may show her the "magic marbles" morning. Let her carry hers, the red one. Let it make her happy too. She will understand the language of the other children too. She's going to be happy when she plays their games and understand them too, "TM said softly in Peter's mind.

Peter had put the blue in the sac again and put him in his pocket.

"Nobody else but you and I can know about me, Peter. Understand? The camel said.

"Yes, TM, " Peter said back to the camel from his mind.

"About the question of the children in your mind, they will come with us for some time. Then, I'm going to help them find their families too. Don't you worry for them for when the time comes and I'm going to send each where they belong? I've got a very special game for them to send them home. Each will have to ride on my back too one time even if only a moment and call my name three times with a wish, " Tal-Mishem said to Peter speaking to his mind. Peter listened to Tal-Mishem and knew all would be well for the other children also.

"Sarah, Peter said, "look at the other children are not crying. You have to be brave too Sarah. Remember what Mr. Bernard said about being brave? Mom and dad are going to find us soon. They're looking for us with troops from the Royal Crown and they will find us when we get to Egypt for sure," Peter said to Sarah sobbing a bit.

"Peter, said TM, "tell Sarah her mom and dad are coming with royal troops. In a week or two, they're going to be around us. Peter's eyes gleamed with happiness. The caravan rested that night by the lake. Then, just as planned by Tal-Mishem, he talked to the thieves in their heads. He confused every one of them as planned. He talked to the head of the chief. The chief of thieves turned pale and threatened the man next to him.

"What did you just said to me? Smelly old goat! The chief said upset to the man next to him and his best friend.

"I looked at you for some time. You indeed look like a donkey, hahaha! The man said laughing at the chief.

"And you look like a hippo, fat and ugly! The Chief of the thieves shut back upset.

"Oh, really? Then, I would look like your wife; she's fat and round as an elephant," the other man replied. They went back and forth getting into an argument.

Minutes later, they wanted to go sleep instead. Chief of the thieves got up and went inside his tent. Hearing enough of the man he went to sleep, but before he ordered.

"Everybody gets to sleep! Tomorrow we're going to travel early!! He shouted upset and left to his tent. The other men following their chief orders went to sleep too. When they went to sleep, Tal- Mishem put his second plan in action. When all the men fell asleep his plan began. He sent messages to the sleeping men's heads. Tal-Mishem told Peter to talk to the children to prepare for their escape. TalMishem helped Peter and he spoke to the children and they understood him well.

By midnight, Peter and Sarah woke up the children and all mounted their camels ready to escape. Tal-Mishem put more heavy dreams in the thieves' heads and they never heard a sound the camels made. Then, one by one all the children got ready to travel.

Tal-Mishem went down on his front legs for Peter and Sarah to climb to his back and leading the other children into their escape. In the sky above, a full moon seemed to follow them throwing its pale light over the sands of the desert. Then, later around they stopped and Peter asked two of the children to jump to his camel and they did repeating three times Tal-Mishem's name.

The all the children mounted on the back of Tal-Mishem for a moment and one by one, they all jumped off from is back to their camels again. After that, nobody felt sleepy or tired. They all felt very happy. They traveled for many miles singing and feeling merry. The moon above them seemed bigger and rounder than ever. Its pale, silver face lighted their way and the camel walked on and on without complaining of being tired or being thirsty. It's like magic Peter told himself and TM winked at him with a grin in its face. When the moon went home and the sun rose again, they went across the border.

They've traveled through Tunisia and Libya passing by many towns and villages. They've seen green mountains and lakes.

Lakes of salt and a lot more they had never imagined existed anywhere. Sometime later, Tal-Mishem asked Peter to tell the children they were stopping for some time and they did and rested. Then, the caravan came to a small Oasis in the middle of nowhere for them to quench their thirst and sleep under the shade of the Oasis trees.

Tal-Mishem asked Peter and all the children to take a good nap. They would travel again at nighttime and stay away from the heat of the afternoon sun. They all cuddled and went to sleep while TalMishem knelt on its belly and looked after them. They slept until evening and traveled under the moon again.

Chapter Twelve
Entering Khufu

When all the children had sat on Tal-Mishem's back, Peter could hear him talking to them. His words entering their minds one by one as he told them about his own adventures while in the desert. The children heard in wonder the fantastic tales and old stories while traveling, but the last was about the life of Tal-Mishem in its own nation, a far, far away constellation. He caught the attention of the children as the White Camel relayed the story, word by word, to all the children, right inside their heads.

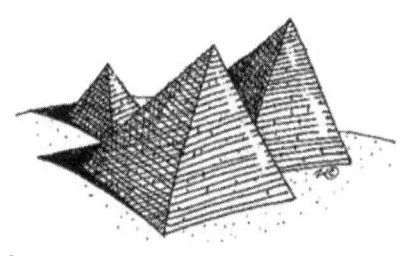

"I was just a little a very young camel going from here to there when all this happened to me; yes, it may sound sometimes incredible, but believe me it was so," pronounced Tal-Mishem in his deep, soothing voice entered their heads.

They all heard the first part of that story from the White Speaking Camel. "I walked then on my way home when I from somewhere, from a nearby forest perhaps, a tall animal, much taller than me, showed on my way. Looking at him carefully I told myself he was not a camel or giraffe or elephant either, or any other animal that I knew.

"But he seemed friendly and spoke very subtle, calling me by my name and telling me, look beyond Tal-Mishem, see those worlds below? I said yes and somehow, I could see everything in those worlds. Everything I did see then seemed wonders and immediately wanted to see them with my own eyes.

"I didn't think anything about its false charm. I wanted to travel to those worlds, I said and the animal in front of me said, "my friend, do not worry all you have to do is just go through the unseen door. If you so desire, you'll be down there anytime and come back here when you want," he said and I believed every word, but the animal never told me about the peril that I might never return to my home. When I thought about it, he dared me."

"Are you perhaps too afraid of your own decisions," the unknown animal challenged me. I was bothered, I was not a coward, I told him and myself, and then chose to go through the door; perhaps ignoring wise words from my parents reminding me to be prudent. I was too late by then and I felt down on and on. The next thing, I found myself in the middle of the desert here. That's my story and now I needed to discover the door back to my constellation, but I think I'm going in a good direction, my heart tells me so," said Tal-Mishem speaking to the children as he had promised to Peter and Sarah.

That evening, when the moon went home and the sun rose again, Peter and the other children traveled across the border into Egypt. They went from Tunisia to Libya through villages and lakes as well as green mountains.

Also, they had seen the unimaginable cities and villages; some small and some large. Plenty of everything and more they had never imagined existed anywhere. Sometime later, Tal-Mishem asked Peter to tell children that they stopped and rested when the caravan came to a small Oasis in the middle of nowhere; they quench their thirst and rest their bodies.

Tal-Mishem made appear food and water out nowhere for all the children. Again Tal-Mishem said to all children to take a nap. They would travel again at night and would be kept away from the heat of the sun and other crooks in the desert seeking children to enslave.
All lie down and went to sleep under the shade of the trees of the Oasis while Tal-Mishem watched over them.

They slept until midnight and traveled under the moon again. When the sun rose the next morning the pyramids of Giza were sighted at the distance. From that far they looked like giant triangles. Later they went through the city of Giza where children would be made free to return home again. They all jumped off their camels and had for breakfast plenty of camel's milk and pita bread.

They were asked to sleep after breakfast and prepare for that afternoon. So, they played the game until tire the fell asleep for a few hours under the guarding of Tal-Mishem. And later in the evening, it was time to go again. Late that night, they left Giza and went around on the skirt of the city and into the desert again.

The pyramids stood like the wonders Peter and Sarah had seen in the books. One looked the tallest of all; that's where a king and Pharaoh of Egypt rested, and people called Khufu and sometimes Keops too. Then another in the middle not too tall called Kafhre and also one not too tall people called Menkaure not too far from villages.

Khufu? What kind of name is that? Sarah asked when Peter told her the name of the tallest pyramid.

"Khufu was the name of a king. They called their kings Pharaohs and Pharaohs thought the river Nile sacred. All life depended on its water. In old times, the river Nile turned into a 'red river'. It became a red river that nobody could drink from it. People and animals died.
One day its waters became clear again," Tal-Mishem said.

"How did the waters turn red? Sarah asked curiously.

"Yes, Tal-Mishem, please tell me how this large river turned red," Peter asked too.

"Nobody knows exactly but the story-tellers only say it was the Pharaoh's fault. He was punished for he was not a kind man.
"He held many slaves and his people were poor and hungry. The river turned into red waters until he let them free, Tal-Mishem said. "Why they built the Pyramids," Sarah asked Peter.

"Well, father says they were houses for the Pharaohs after they died," Peter said.

"The Pharaohs believe they would be kings after dying. Before dying they asked their slaves to build those pyramids, "Peter answered.

"But they are very big to build. How many bricks did they use for building them?

"I can answer that Peter if you want me? Tal-Mishem asked Peter.

"Yes, I don't know this answer," Peter said.

"Well, historians think Egyptians used millions of large bricks. They took many years to build them, Sarah. Maybe more than thirty years. They cut large stones to make bricks. They moved bricks up to the sides to build the pyramids. They might have been thousands of men working day and night. Many were carpenters. Other carried water. Others were engineers and architects. Others were mathematicians who knew numbers," Peter said.

"Did our dad tell you about these historians too? Sarah asked. "He let me read it in his books," Peter said proudly. Then Tal-Mishem spoke to Peter again.

"Peter do exactly as I tell you. You and Sarah will mount on my back. We're going to travel together through the night. Then we're going to travel for one day. We're going to hide for a day or two, but before t that we're sending the children home. After two days or so, we're going to travel to Cairo," TM added.

Peter said yes and Tal-Shem heard him clearly. Peter and Sarah were holding the giggling marbles now. The village on the side of Giza showed far, far away that afternoon.

The three pyramids stood in the distance as small triangles. But soon they turned larger and taller as they got closer by late that evening and moonlight felt over them.

"The tallest is the Great Pyramid and the Pyramid of Cheops is in the middle. Then, Khufu is the smallest, "Tal-Mishem said to the children.

The village in Khufu was made of yellowish houses. They look brighter under the sun. Each house seemed pushed against each other. Peter thought of a giant beehive in the middle of the desert. Then in the middle of the village an open market that welcomed people. The camels followed the narrow streets. The animals moved patiently. A few lanky street dogs stood barking at the camels. Slaughtered animals hung in the open ready to be cooked. They saw along the road, chicken, ducks, and geese.

Shop keepers offered their goods with loud voices to visitors. Seated between the humps on Tal-Mishem back Peter and Sarah enjoyed the view of the market. Their eyes explored it all. They saw street peddlers and carpet makers and children offering the wares. Everything looked so fantastic as if coming from the pages of Aladdin's tales, Peter told himself as fantasy paraded now in front of his very own eyes. A talking came, he said. A band of desert bandits, he though.

A journey through the melting dessert and everything seemed so unreal. All could be just a dream, he thought many times. A figment of my imagination, Peter thought. But until then, nothing could be more real for him and his sister now rode on the back of a talking camel. Nothing could be more real than heading to an unknown place. A land that a few days before only existed in the pages of a book and they were there now. The narrow, dirt street ended at the mouth of a huge bazaar. It looked like a large store covered by a high round roof and highest than any building in London, Peter thought.

The roof windows above let the glow of light into the market. Smoke danced along with thick vapor floating around. There were kitchens and places to eat inside. There were boiling cauldrons and cooks. Inside it felt cool and offered shade from the sun. Sometime later, a man came to the children offered the pita bread. Peter ate his and like it a lot. They are yummy he said to Sarah. Sarah refused to eat. That evening Peter shared his pita bread with Tal-Mishem.

"Ahah, it is delicious! I love this stuff, "Tal-Mishem said biting and chewing on the last crumbles left in his mouth.

"Thank you, Peter! You don't know how much I have craved one of these. Pita reminds me of a good pizza pie just a bit smaller. What I would give love for a pie of pizza too. I had a few of them in my last days in Italy, " Tal-Mishem said making Peter feel even hungrier. Have you traveled to Italy too? Peter asked surprised.

"Yeah, of course, a long time ago. But that's another story. I'm going to tell you all about it when we travel through the desert. Oh, Italy is beautiful and I keep it close to my heart. Oh, I love their music! Their tenors, oh Peter If could sing like one of them. And above all, I love the Gondolas in Venice going through streets of water! TM said remembering.

"Have you gone to China yet? Peter asked curiously now.

"Oh, China yes Peter. It reminds a lot about my own Gran Oasis! The old China Wall never ends. Its beautiful mountains are different than any others anywhere; the famous Great Wall is over five thousand miles long.

"Built many centuries ago too! It goes through mountains as tall as Tibet itself. I'm ready to go back there anytime and walk on the walk from one end to the other, " Tal-Mishem said happily.

"Was the wall also made by Pharaohs? Sara asked.

"No, of course not Sarah. The Chinese wall was built by Chinese emperors!
Most of it was built by the Emperor of the Qin-Shi-Huang dynasty. It was built in his own time about seven hundred years ago. Before England became a country. Even before Europe and America existed for China is a very, very old nation, " Tal-Mishem said.

"Wow! You sound like you've traveled around. I would love to do that too, " Peter said amused to hear from Tal-Mishem had traveled far visiting all countries around the world.

"I'm getting hungry again, Tal-Mishem said thinking about pitabread and Peter read the message in his head.

"I'm still holding to one, Peter said to Tal-Mishem and they stopped.

"The word pita is a Greek name for flattened, "Tal-Mishem said biting at his pita.

"I like them...too. They sort of tasty, "Peter said.

"Giving them some away to travelers is an old custom. You see, each traveler resting under the bazaar is expected to buy something from the local shoppers.

"It is done in return for the shoppers' being kind offering their shade under the dome," explained Tal-Mishem again. When the sun rays have gone, it was time to sleep again. Peter and Sarah lay down on camels' pellets to rest sleep again.

"Peter? Said Sarah softly. She was thinking about Mr. Bernard's words back in London.

"What Sarah? Peter answered half-sleeping already.

"Maybe, but will know when we wake up tomorrow," Peter said and hugged Sarah and they closed their eyes.

That night beautiful dreams waited for Peter and Sarah. When he finally fell asleep, they traveled to China and walked on the Great Wall of China. From there they went to see the old Roman Coliseum in Italy and from there to the Taj-Mahal palace in India too.

Then, as they flew and visited many other countries. All his traveling on the back of the White Talking Camel, in their dreams, of course.

Chapter Thirteen
Giggling Marbles

Peter sat on the sand close to Tal-Mishem and the soothing voice of Tal-Mishem entered his head and they talked again. He turned to the camel as he heard him speak to him. The night had fallen over them. I want to go home, Sarah whispered amongst sobs and tears on her face. Her round blue eyes gleamed with wetness reflecting the pale blue moonlight above them.

"Don't worry Peter and tell Sarah not to be sad. In a few days, we're very far from the thieves. They have no camels, "Tal-Mishem spoke mentally to Peter.

The brother and sister cuddled together and got ready to sleep. The cool wind reminded Peter of London. Minutes later the rapid cold of the desert fell over them. Two of the oldest children walked around the herd of camels picking up the dried dung and the dropped it into the fire. A dance of flames rose into the air in a whirlpool of sparks.

Sarah began counting the floating sparks. Peter's eyes followed with interest the twister of sparks going up the sky like fireflies. The next morning before Peter could come to awake himself, he felt Sarah's hand pushing him to wake up. The cool morning still hovered over them, but Sarah seemed quite awake.

"Peter, listen to Pete...I have just dreamed of the camel too! The Talking Camel was in my dream too.....it was so real I didn't want to wake up Peter! Peter, wake up! Sarah said pushing Peter to wake up. It was morning already.

"I know Sarah. He said he would come to you too. We're going home, right? Peter asked and Sarah's eyes got rounder and bigger.

"Yeah...she said. He said that too," Sarah confirmed.

"I know Sarah. Tal-Mishem asked me to tell you. He's here to help us escape and even though you have only heard his voice, he's here, " Peter mumbled in a whisper.

"Is that his name? It sounds like you said "Paul Misshem". It's a weird name. Can we just call him Mr. Camel instead?

"I like it too, Peter said. We can ask Tal-Mishem, but he likes TM. Tall means sleepy camel, he told me for a baby he loves to sleep more than all camels, " Peter said softly, and Sarah giggled on that.

"I have an idea! Why don't we call him Paul-Mishem? It rhymes with Tal. See Paul and Tal they sound the same. I can remember that easy, "Sarah said giggling.

"I don't know. He might like his real name more than an English name. Look Peter said, he pushed a hand into his pocket. Here...these are the magic marbles. They will make you giggle when you put them in your hands."

"Try it...now, "Peter said putting the marbles on Sarah's tiny hand who grabbed the marble.

"What do I do now Peter...they make happy," Sarah said giggling and feeling happy again.

"Say something..say good morning Tal-Mishem this Sarah. He'll hear you for sure, "Peter said and Sarah did.

"Good morning...Mr. Tal-Mishem," Sarah said and giggled feeling funny.

"Good morning, Sarah and to you Peter. It's a wonderful day. We have a long way to go. Be ready. Please, Sarah, get some milk and eat your pita bread. You're going to need all your strength when we travel the desert again," Tal-Mishem said with a friendly voice.

They were ready to go. Peter brought Sarah the pouch filled with camel's milk. Sarah took a large drink from the pouch, then a second one. She smacked her lips pleased with the camel's milk for the first time. Peter put a large squirt in his mouth too.

"Not bad, ahh Sarah? Asked Tal-Mishem.

"Great, Tal-Mishem, thank you.....it doesn't taste greasy...anymore. I'm going to have it every morning from now on," Sarah said. After breakfast and on the camel's back Sarah begged Peter if she could use the magic marble.

"Tal-Mishem calls them Marbles", Peter explained as Sarah giggled about the marbles' new name.

"I call them gigglers for they make giggle," Sarah said looking closer at the white transparency of the marbles.

"Think only what you want to say," Peter said happy to see her sister's face glowing with happiness.

"They tickled me! They tickled a lot! Sarah said giggling again and again. Once on the hump of Tal-Mishem and her arms around his brother, Sarah talked to Tal-Mishem again. A million questions popped in her head as the caravan walked into the sands. Sarah was giggling again holding the magic marbles. "They make me giggle so much," Sarah said enjoying the tickling marbles.

"Ok, Peter, it's fine, let her be happy again," Tal-Mishem said to Peter. The camels were watered, and the caravan moved again. After a while, the trail leading to their destination became a deserted road. It was sprinkled with pebbles and dried yellowish stones of all sizes. Peter and Sarah thought of the false gold of Spain.

They came to a water hole. They rested a bit under some trees. Later the sun lost its heat and the cool of the night fell upon the desert like a very cold blanket while the caravan camped out again. Much later that evening the winds began whistling. Peter and Sarah cuddled against each other under the pelts to stay warm.

"Tal-Mishem...?

"Yes, Peter.

"Do animals feel sad sometimes?

"Are you thinking about the baby camel, Peter," asked Tal-Mishem reading his mind.

"I know what happened that day Peter. The old camel soon will return where he once belonged. He will find happiness among his own kind. Man is sometimes unkind to animals, "Tal-Mishem said with sadness in his voice.

"I wished to have done more and make them free from that man," said Peter.

"I know Peter, but you did. Now pay attention, Peter. The winds will be blowing harder than any other day. When we travel again to keep a firm grip on me and look over Sarah. And you Sarah grab from your brother's waist. It's going to be windy and chilly sometimes early in the morning. And then, very hot again, "Tal-Mishem warned.

The next morning, they left again. Tal-Mishem walked fast and for sometimes it felt like he wasn't walking on the sand, Peter and Sarah noticed. The winds whistled around them and Peter kept a good grip of Tal-Mishem's reins. The morning sun followed them everywhere they went to the desert. Peter and Sarah now had magic marbles to talk to Tal-Mishem.

"This is what Egyptian people call old Egypt. There are many miles from here to the river Nile, "Tal-Mishem said again.

"Where does begin? Peter asked.

"No, tell us where does end, "Sarah also asked.

"Let me tell you, Peter. It begins over six thousand miles from here in a place called Tanzania. Then, it runs through the lands of many countries. People called it the river of all nations too and also the Nile and the Blue Nile for the Blue Nile is found in Lake Tana in the country of Ethiopia, " Tal-Mishem said again.

"Now, listen well Sarah. The Nile river is indeed a mighty river and very old. The river ends in the sea called the Mediterranean where the port of Alexandria is now.

"The old Egyptians always called it the Iter which is the word for river or large channel of water, " Tal-Mishem said stopping for their next question.

"Wow...over six thousand miles...! Pctcr said.

There're more miles than from Cairo to London. Peter said remembering his father said there were two thousand miles from London to Cairo one way and four thousand two ways.

"Indeed, you're correct Peter. Tal-Mishem said.

So, that day, as they went through the desert Peter and Sarah and the Talking camel talked. And talked and talked until sundown.

Tal-Mishem told them about his time in Africa too. Also, he told them about his journey to Australia and Fiji and Tonga.

And of course, without forgetting about his traveling through Japan and Russia as well as other cold, cold lands like Norway and Scandinavia. "But Going to America someday," Tal-Mishem said.

Chapter Fourteen
The Escape to Cairo

Peter and Sarah and Tal-Mishem and the other children gathered around the fire and played many children's games. Thousands of glittering stars covered the sky and many constellations showed clearly for all to see.

Peter and Sarah with the help of Tal-Mishem took their time to tell the children about each of them. They pointed to Aries and Aquarius, then to Cancer the crab and Capricornio the ram, then to Gemini the twins and Leo the lion of the sky. Then Sarah pointed to

Scorpio, then to Taurus the bull and Virgo next to Pisces the little fish in the sky. Indeed, they are too many to count them all, but I hope someday camels can have their own Camel constellation.

"All camels have served well all men, " he said proudly. Peter and Sarah told the children that and they shouted for a camel constellation, yeah, yeah! Peter asked about the river Nile again and Tal-Mishem explained to them about the longest river ever.

"Oh...Peter none more beautiful anywhere in the world. The Great Designer himself shaped it.

"Our great Designer came from the infinity of His kingdom and built all. He built the earth and oceans as well as rivers and mountains. Even the sun and the moon so far away is His design. He spoke to all creations. One by one they all came to be alive. He created animals and plants. The air and the rain they all have a purpose as well.

Day and night were made for men and animals to rest. All perfectly designed for the happiness of all man," Tal-Mishem said to Peter cuddled next to him and others.

"Did the Designer create other rivers as long as the Nile anywhere Tal-Mishem?

"Oh, yes but none runs through so many nations. None gives so much life to so many people," Tal-Mishem said.

Peter listened as his eyes fell on Tal-Mishem knelt down a few yards from him. Peter's fair skin contrasted against the copper hue of his hair. The dancing flames of the fire like pieces of his golden hair. Tal-Mishem laughed. He remembered children had nicknamed his sister Head-on-fire for the reddish color of his hair.

"What Peter asked as Tal-Mishem stared at his hair?

"Do you know the children call you Golden-nugget-head because of the golden color of your hair Peter, "Tal-Mishem said sending the message to Peter's head. Peter giggled as he heard his nickname amongst the children.

"In a day or two Peter, when we enter in Giza we're going across the Nile and then up to Cairo, "Tal-Mishem said.

So, that evening when Peter finished feeding the camels, he quickly returned and sat around the circle with the children. With the help of the magic marbles, Peter spoke to other children. Everyone was told they would go home soon. The children listened in awe as Peter spoke to them from the distance. They all understood each word-thought Peter sent to their heads. Each word sent out via the force of the magic spheres. The children gathered around the fire and played. Then they Peter and Sarah told them the White Talking Camel was there with them. The children's eyes grew larger as they heard that. Many thought the White Talking Camel was a fairy tale only. The moon seemed brighter. Its light shone like never before. Then, TalMishem walked to the center of the fire.

When they went through the market outside of the city, Tal-Mishem looked for a place to hide. He found an old barn outside the village.

It looked abandoned. It didn't have a door or any of its windows; it looked perfect to hide inside and Peter and Sarah on Tal-Mishem's back went inside and hid. Once in there Tal-Mishem gave them instructions again for the next day.

"We're going all to rest for the rest of the day. We've traveled most of the night. We need to sleep a few hours before another trip. We also need to take with us food and water. We're all going to sleep here for tonight," TM said to children.

Sometime later Tal-Mishem and the children went to sleep. Peter and Sarah cuddled next to each other and on the warm and cozy belly of Tal-Mishem to fill warmer in the cold of the night.

"Are we going back home soon, Peter?

"Very soon Sarah, very soon I'm sure. Close your eyes and go to sleep, "Peter said.

"Are mom and dad looking for us? Sarah asked worriedly.

"Yes Sarah, of course, they are looking for us," Peter said.

"Do you think TM knows if they're coming? Can we talk to him? Can we ask him now! Peter let's talk to TM and ask him, "Sarah said aloud trying to keep Peter awake.

"Camels get tired too. Maybe he doesn't want to talk to us now Sarah, "Peter said.

"Camels don't get tired. Camels can walk long distances without food or water and never get tired, "Sarah said.

"We're going to talk to Tal-Mishem tomorrow Sarah. Look at him! His eyes are already closed. He's sleeping now. Let's leave him alone, "Peter asked Sarah.

Sarah stared at the camel for a few seconds. A loud purr sound left Tal-Mishem lips. He was sleeping and snoring aloud like a large cat. "He's sleeping. I'll talk to him tomorrow," Sarah said aloud.

Chapter Fifteen
The Beggar's Gold

Peter and Sarah's words were heard above them. There was a man hiding; a homeless man staying in the old barn too. He had remained hidden in the loft of the roofless house, and he heard the children speak.

He was sleeping before the children came, but then he heard them talking and dragged his body to the edge of the loft. The old beggar heard all about the children and Tal-Mishem, the White Talking Camel! He stared at the children from his hiding place and his eyes looked for the camel. He repeated Sarah's words to himself.

"I'm going ride on him, and I'm going to be is Master," the beggar whispered to himself. The children said they talk to the camel, he told himself many times over. There was no doubt in his mind this was the "talking camel", and if he did ride him, he told himself, the camel would grant him three wishes too.

He repeated the camel's name again and again. He needed to remember the camel's name. He moved his head sideways and took a peek at Tal-Mishem snoring aloud. The man hid once more, but he had noticed the camel's fur; it seemed to glow a soft light the darkness of the room. A white-bluish tint covered his glossy coat like light from the moon above and he looks tall and strong, he reminded himself.

"It's indeed the talking camel! He whispered that to himself one more time and many more remembering all about the tale of the Talking Camel. I'm going to be a rich man now he thought as the beggar repeated the camel's name three times.

Just after that, he thought about his wishes; he went on to think about jewels and palaces, about land and slaves' wishes and many more thoughts came and went through his mind keeping him awake.

Tal-Mishem! Tal-Mishem! He told himself rehearsing the name only two times afraid the camel could hear him now. Make me a king, a very rich king, he practiced in his mind on and on and how to say it. I can't forget his name. All I need is a trick to ride on his back, he thought. He wanted to sleep but his eyes would not close afraid to lose the camel from his sight remembering the old, old story of the talking camel. He needed to ride on its loins even if only once. He rubbed his eyes once and twice and many more times. He shook his head in disbelief.

And again, every now and then, slowly he moved his head to peek again. Tal-Mishem was sleeping deeply, he could tell hearing TalMishem snoring loud with large puffs of air going out along short whistling going through his flaring nostrils. Next to his large furry belly, the beggar could see the children sleeping cuddled next to the camel's belly.

"Ahh, the talking camel! I'm going to be a very rich man from now on. I could be a king too, but gold is enough for me. The old beggar told himself again and again. The tale of the white talking camel returned to his head.

He tried to sleep but stayed awake thinking that as a child he had dreamed of finding the camel too. Now, he is there, he said to himself. He needed a trick, he thought. He needed a plan to ride on the camel's hump. He would be granted whatever he wanted If I could ride on the camel's back and all is going to fine If I only do that, he reminded himself. Even if only for one second, he thought and he laid down staying awake all night long. He thought about this and that wish. He would ask Tal-Mishem a palace. Yeah. One made of white marble and golden domes like the Taj-Mahal in India.

Then, he thought about gems and gold filling many coffers. Then, he thought about land and a thousand slaves. Yes, the endless land of abundant vineyards and many slaves.

He perhaps wanted a large herd of camels. Yeah, he pondered for some time. Ten thousand camels would make rich too, he thought. I want to be a Sheik. No, not that! A king instead, he told himself thinking about what he could ask the camel. He could not wait for the next day. He dreamed of being like the king of Damascus. Maybe the one in Bagdad, he went on and on. But then he thought about being a Pharaoh.

"Yes, that's it, a Pharaoh is richer than any king, " he told himself in a whisper. He stayed thinking awake the whole night. When the sun came out again and he was awake. The camel and the children were together and talked. Later, Peter and Sarah left early in the morning.

They went and helped around the market. To earn a few Shekels for they needed money. For one day the children labored in the market. They fed and watered camels. They ran errands for tired travelers. They made the dough for pita bread. They work hard and honestly. They earned enough for food and water. The trip back to Cairo only a few days away through the desert.

In the meantime, the beggar followed the children. He kept an eye on them thinking about his own plan. He needed to climb on the camel's back to be his master. He stayed hidden in the old barn. He listened to Peter and Sarah. He knew all about Tal-Mishem and about the English children's kidnap and escape. For sure he knew it was the talking camel.

"Oh, poor child! Somebody help him! He shouted to himself aloud. He faked the most terrible grief sitting and crying in a corner of the abandoned barn. Poor, poor child! The beggar cried out for TalMishem and Sarah to hear him and they did and came to him with pity.

"What's the matter, old man? Why are you crying? What makes you so sad? Sarah asked him with kindness. The man pointed towards the market saying. "They all are thieves to me.

"They're looking for a child in the market. There is a kid in need of help. His name is Peter. He asked to look for Sarah his sister, he needs help!

He said pretending grief again. If I could only walk, the beggar said with tears in his eyes. He wanted Tal-Mishem to hear him. The man sounded sincere. His words sounded truthful and Tal-Mishem forgot being careful with himself. Tal-Mishem forgot that nobody should ride on his back or would be his Master. Nobody, except kind and brave children he would carry on him. If somebody rode on his back, it would be his master and a new master could demand three wishes from him or never let him go free again.

"They're going to take the kid! They're going to take him away. They're going to find him. He's hiding behind the carpets shop," he said faking his worry.

"We have to help him! Tal-Mishem said ready to go.

"I would, the beggar said, but I am very old. My legs are weak and I cannot walk the distance to the market. I would need a mare or donkey, "the beggar said.

"Sarah said Tal-Mishem; his voice firm. You stay Sarah, stay here. I'll carry this old man on my back. It is a short distance anyway TalMishem said the camel and went down on his front legs. The beggar quickly climbed to Tal-Mishem's back. Wait for us here! "Don't come outside at any time, "Tal-Mishem yelled to Sarah.

My trick has worked, the beggar thought and picked the reins as he left the barn behind and the camel took quick steps. They went looking for Peter, but then Tal-Mishem heard the beggar yelling at his ear.

"I'm your master now! Hahhhahaaah, You must grant me now my three wishes," the beggar said laughing aloud.

"I'm on your back. And I am your new master for I know also your name. Tal-Mishem, Tal-Mishem, Tal-Mishem!!

Grant me three wishes, is my command for that's your name and I know it," the beggar said the camel's name three times repeating, I'm your master now! With that, his new master could ask him three wishes to be granted to him.

Chapter Sixteen
Ambitious Beggar

The old man's eyes glittered with ambition. A glow of happiness rushed to his face. He saw himself on top of the camel as a king. He was now the new Master of the White Talking Camel, he told himself with pride.

"Grant my wishes now," he commanded the beggar.

"I grant all your three wishes Master, but please let me walk to the market and find the boy. He's like my little brother to me. If I can't find him, your wishes I might not grant to you for my heart my not talk to my mind. If I can't find him, your wishes I might not grant to you because my heart will be too sad, and I may die before, "TalMishem said feeling weak already.

The beggar said okay, and they went to look for Peter. It took TalMishem only a few minutes to walk to the market. Its big brown eyes looked everywhere for Peter, but before he could find him, the beggar demanded his wishes again. He grabbed the camel's reins shouting aloud.

"No more of this nonsense, this is my wish," he said upset to Tal-Mishem. "Get me down! I command you! I know you are a talking camel and I'm your new Master, obey me now! The beggar demanded and Tal-Mishem put him down.

"And now grant me three wishes. You cannot deny them to me. I have heard you talking to the boy and the girl!

"I know your name too. I said Tal-Mishem three times too. I have ridden on your back as the story says," the beggar demanded, and TalMishem went down as ordered. The man went down holding to the reins.

"Talk to me camel! I order you that you talk to me! I am your Master now, and I've mounted on you back too! The beggar shouted and demanded to hear the camel's talk.

"Yes, you are my Master now. Tal-Mishem said talking to the man moving his lips. "But I only have a wish left for you," Tal-Mishem reminded his new Master.

"What? You must grant me three wishes. Only one is a trick! You're worse than a thief and scoundrels in the bazaar! The beggar yelled at Tal-Mishem.

"I've granted you two wishes already Master. First, you commanded me to get you down and I did. Second, you commanded me to talk to you. I'm doing that now. That's wish number two," Tal-Mishem eyes looked at the man patiently and spoke kindly to the beggar. "Yes, you are my Master now. If you remember the riddle well," explained TalMishem patiently, "I can only grant three wishes. You only have one left now. Think fast because there is no time left; soon, the king of Egypt and his men will be around. He wants me for his herd and kingdom and your head may roll with his ire. He'll put me in his gardens. People will come and see me talking and they're going to laugh at me. People will have fun with my talking, but I won't be free but you will end up in dungeon too! Tal-Mishem reminded the beggar.

The old beggar stood upset in front of Tal-Mishem for some time. Not knowing what to ask from the camel he paced from here to there. He thought and thought for some time. For many years and now he could wish the pain to go away.

"Help me then. You are older and wiser," asked the old man. What would be better from my last wish? The man begged from TalMishem because the old beggar man could not decide for himself. "Wish to be a good and fortune seek your way in many ways," Tal-Mishem said. "No, not that! I want the richness of gold coins, the power of kings and their armies, "he shouted impatiently and confused.

He had always wished to be rich. He didn't know what to ask. He could ask for gold.

"You could ask you for gold, but what would you do with gold when you cannot walk?

"I could ask you to cure me of my pain. But then I would be poor again! I don't want to be a pauper without any of the gold! The beggar yelled upset with himself.

"I can only grant your wishes. I cannot tell you what to wish for," Tal-Mishem said softly.

"Very well, then. Make me rich like a king, fill my pocket with dinars of gold until they flow like a river! Said the beggar requesting his last wish.

"As you wish Master," Tal-Mshem said ready to do as commanded.

"Fill the pockets of my garments! Fill them until gold coins are many and flow out of them like water from the river Nile! The ambitious old beggar commanded and Tal-Mishem granted him the worse of his wishes.

"If that is your wish, your wish will be granted now! Tal-Mishem said.

Then, Tal-Mishem closed his round eyes. He granted the third and last wish for the beggar. Soon gold coins filled the old beggar's garments pockets. Large golden coins flowed out from his pockets like water. He tried to stop them! The river of gold coins rushed out even more. The coins flowed out of the beggar's garments like a river indeed.

Clicking, link, link, link, they sounded as each fell to the ground and rolled around. The old beggar went crazy. He jumped and danced as the gold coins filled the pockets of his garments.

But gold coins kept falling to the ground. Gold coins falling from the old man flowing even more and more. Then, mobs of people ran to him. Men, women, and children yelling gold coins, gold coins! Beggars and merchants ran for the coins. Even old and sick people like him. All came to pick the coins of gold. They all ran after the gold coins. The coins rolled around him just like he had wished.

Like the river Nile flowing everywhere. The coins kept falling and rolling. Each coin chased by children and men. Everybody went running to pick the falling coins. Link, link, link, the coins sounded falling and rolling to everybody's feet.

Gold coins! Gold coins are falling from the old beggar clothes! The voices filled the market. Come and get the coins falling from his garments! People shouted and more people ran to pick up the coins falling. "Gold coins falling for all! The more people shouted the more people rushed to pick the beggar's coins.

A lot of people rushed to pick up the coins coming out from the beggar's garments. The old beggar tried to stop them. He could not walk fast enough to getaway. He would stop the coins from one pocket and then gold coins would flow from one and the other pocket!

"Getaway, getaway!! Get away from my gold coins! You scoundrels!

He yelled. But more coins flowed out from the next. He screamed and pushed men, women, and children. He screamed at beggars. They all laughed at him. Beggars and merchants ran to him with sacs. They filled one and two and three with gold coins from the beggar's pockets. But after some time, the gold coins flow stopped running. Many people holding gold coins laughed at the old beggar. People now rich laughed at him. They went happy with many gold coins in their pockets. But the old beggar became very sad. He left the market limping from the pain on his legs.

"I've full-filled your wishes, old man. You should never speak of me again. If you do much harm may come to you. Hear my warning. Go in peace and do no more harm to yourself.

Look for your leg before you look for gold or shall suffer much more pain, " Tal-Mishem said warning the old beggar. The old beggar walked away in shame as poor as before.

"Tal-Mishem, Tal-Mishem....! Peter yelled running toward him.

"What happened? Asked Peter mentally and Tal-Mishem explained.

Then, Tal-Mishem walked back to the abandoned barn with Peter on his back and new master again. Sarah waited for them. Peter told Sarah about the old beggar's trick. Then Tal-Mishem said to them that granting three wishes in one day would make him very tired. His fur would get old and lose its glow. He needed to rest before going into the desert again. So, Tal-Mishem lay down to rest for a while Peter and Sarah looked after him kindly.

"Can you grant us three wishes too? Asked Sarah.

"Yes, Sarah. In time I will grant you three wishes. Also for you Peter. You have ridden on my back and know my name. But above you're kind and brave, "TM said.

"Now, listen very well. Tomorrow we have to go back to the market and buy the goods we need for the desert trip. Sarah will ride on my back. You, Peter, will lead me by the reins, "Tal-Mishem said tired and talked the children again. You'll do the buying and the haggling. I tell you what to buy and what price to pay, "Tal-Mishem instructed the children. Peter nodded. The next day, the camel and the children left their hiding place. The three wandered through the narrow streets of the city. They bought food and water for the desert trip to Cairo.

Chapter Seventeen
The Beggar and the Cook

The old beggar went crying his misfortune and wandered through the city. He walked the streets and by night came to sleep right behind the walls of the king's palace. He woke up next morning dying of hunger. He smelled the odor of food that escaped from the king's kitchen. He peeked through the window hoping to get a handout from the cook yelling out to the cook inside.

"Please feed me only once. I'll tell you a secret. It will make you the favorite servant of the king," the beggar said aloud for the cook to hear him. The cook stopped his chores for a second. He went and stared at the beggar who was outside looking through a tiny window of the palace.

"And what could be more important than the king's food? I am already his favorite cook. I travel with him everywhere he goes! The cook said with true pride.

But the beggar did not let himself be discouraged. He was very hungry by then and said.

"You surely are his favorite cook. Hear my secret and you'll want to feed me then!

"Surely I will make you his favorite servant more than now. If you only feed me once from the King's food, even the dog's leftovers if you want," said the beggar.

"Tell me your secret now and feed you after! Demanded the cook with a threat in his words.

"No, I cannot tell you before you feed me. I am so weak that surely I would die before I finish my story," said the beggar faking stomach hunger pains and the cook fixed his round eyes on the man. The beggar's words touched his ambition too and he let the old man come inside to eat.

"I'll feed you once and only once, old man. I'll cook you myself if you're lying. The king may cut my head if I were to lie to him too! The cook said.

"Allah will bless you for your kindness. After, I tell you my secret. You will not mind feeding me once and for the rest of your life," said the beggar.

The old man ate under the suspicious eyes of the black cook. When he finished the cook demanded the secret. The old beggar recited the story. He told him all about the children and the talking camel. The tall, big cook stood up. His angry eyes fell on the beggar. Then he picked up the old man. He walked to the door threw him in the air.

The old beggar landed in a pile of garbage outside the palace walls. The cook threatened to cook him alive. The old man left the walls of the palace before the cook could do as he yelled out.

"I should have known better you old crook! Shouted the cook closing the door.

But the story of the talking camel and children went around and around. Like many rumors, it didn't stop with the cook. It went from the cook's mouth to many others. It went from the cooking maids to the elephants-keeper. Then it went from him to the king's gardens keepers. Then, it went from them to the maids in the king's quarters.

A few days later, the king himself heard the rumors of the talking camel. The king called each and every one of his servants. He asked them about the story. The maids claimed they had heard the story from the captain of guards. The guards, in turn, claimed to have heard the story from the elephants-keeper. The elephants-keeper, in turn, said he had heard the story from the gardener who heard from kitchen maids. The king ordered the Captain of the guard to bring the cook to him. The cook man came to the king. He knelt afraid for his life in front of him.

"Do you know that beggar from the camel story?

"No mighty king. He tricked me to feed him. Then told me about two children and the talking camel in Giza? The cook said.

"Do you know where to find him?

"No mighty king, but he's an old man who begs in the market," the cook added.

"Can you recognize his face if you find him again?

"As well as I know you are my king," the cook replied with respect.

"Very well, go with a man or two from my guard. Find this beggar and don't come back to the palace without him! Put him in a dungeon! Ordered the King. Just as Tal-Mishem had forewarned the beggar never to speak again of him that harm would come to the old man. The servants left the king room frightened by the ruler's threats. Minutes later the captain of the guards led a group of fifty men. Galloping on fast the horsemen left the palace to look for the beggar and the camel everywhere. That night Peter and Sarah and Tal-Mishem left to the desert again. Peter, remembering Tal-Mishem promise to tell them where he came from, asked Tal-Mishem the question again.

"Tal-Mishem, where do you come from? Asked Peter in a whisper thought that went to the camel's mind clearly.

"Ah! That's a long, long story, Peter. I have not forgotten my promise.

"Would you tell us now then?

"Is that your wish? Yeah, said Peter and Sarah in their minds.

"Well, I don't know if I should. Maybe some other time, TalMishem said.

"Please Tal-Mishem! We're your friends. We promise not to tell anybody else!

"Please begged Peter and Sarah again.

"Let me think, uhmm, where do I begin?

Tal-Mishem said making the children's faces glow with curiosity.

In the meantime, not too far from them, the king's men were looking everywhere for them.

Chapter Eighteen
The Mathematician

The king called the Captain of his guards and shouted his orders. Soon after that, the king's men left to find the old mathematician who knew the riddle of the Talking Camel. "Tell him to bring all his celestial maps. Without them, he won't ever see his daughter! Tell him to come with you, if he wants to see his daughter ever again, "the king threatened. The captain of the guards left with quick strides while the king paced in the room impatiently. His maids rested on the pillows strewn on the floor behind the king. Jaz-Min stood facing the king. He looked at her with curious eyes.

"Does your father know anything about the "talking camel"? The king questioned Jaz-Min the mathematician's daughter.

"Maybe no more and no less than any others know mighty king, but he is a great mathematician and reads the charts of the skies also. He's a wise man indeed, "Jaz-Min answered the king.

"Why I never heard of him?

"He is a quiet, old man. He worked for your grandfather in his court when you were only a small child," said the maid remembering that from his father.

"You have nothing to fear from me if your father worked in my father's court. Tell me about yourself," the king demanded.

"My father named me Jaz-Min. He says that as a baby I had the fragrance of a flower.

"He thought that I would be as pretty as one, but I am not as pretty as any one of your maids," Jaz-Min told the king attentively listening.

"He's a wise man and a man that can discern beauty too," the king said. "But I guess he is a better mathematician than he is a man that can see the beauty of his own daughter."

Jaz-Min said thank you humbly, lowering her eyes.

"He may not be either. But he certainly is a great seer for you grew to be as beautiful as a flower as he thought so you would be, "the King added.

"You have many beautiful women here," Jaz-Min answered.

"Why I have never seen before this day?

"I work in your kitchen, your majesty. They sent me there for I lacked the beauty of many of your maids in your quarters, "Jaz-Min let the king know.

"Nonsense! You are much prettier than many of my many maids! And as of this day, you'll live in their quarters and shall come to visit me when I request it so!

"Yes, mighty king," said the young Jaz-Min lowering her head and hiding a tear rolling down her cheek for she valued her freedom very much.

The king clapped his hands. A tall and dark servant came into the room. After listening to the king's orders, he left with Jaz-Min. In the meantime, the king horsemen trotted on their way to a small village. They needed to find the house of the old mathematician. The old mathematician heard the orders from the king.

His thoughts went to his daughter. He prepared to leave immediately. He grabbed his celestial charts. He walked outside. He mounted one of the horses waiting for him. Then the captain and his men left the tiny village. A cloud of desert dust rose into the air as the horsemen galloped away.

The sun's rays bathed the palace when the horsemen went through its gates of the palace. They dismounted their horses. The head of the guards led the mathematician to see the king in his quarters. They walked through a large opening at the center of the palace. The atrium looks good, "said the old man to himself. A water fountain stood in the middle. It welcomed all visitors and offered freshness that cooled the king's palace. Good idea too whispered the mathematician to himself again.

He had been the architect of the palace. The old man's eyes wandered everywhere. He felt happy to walk through the gardens of his own design. He looked at the archways facing the atrium. Then, he looked at the cool hallways. He looked at large windows smiling. And of course, he walked the long and tall corridors for cooling the hot air of the desert and smiled again.

His deign had stood the passage of time, he told himself. He thought of the endless days he had worked to make the king's father palace the most beautiful of all. The captain escorting him stopped in front of a giant door. He demanded the two men guarding the doorway to open it. When they passed through the door, the king himself waited for them. The king rested on a set of large floor pillows.

Jaz-Min sat a few feet behind the king. The old man bowed and greeted the ruler, but never looked at his own daughter behind the king amongst the king's many maids.

"Are you the father of this flower you named Jaz-Min old man?

"Yes, I am, mighty king. She is the only fruit of my loins. The greatest gift to me," the old mathematician answered proudly with his head bowed to his king.

"Is it true that you worked in my father's court as well?

"Indeed, I did, great king. I was younger then. You were only a very small child. You may not remember me in the court of grandfather," Jaz-Min father said.

"Are you a mathematician and seer?

"I study the Alge-Bra of our forefathers like many of our wise ancestors. I am nothing but an old, simple man.

"I love numbers since from an early age taught by my father," my king. "And I've learned of the stars and constellation in the distant skies," he answered humbly.

"He's a mathematician and architect too, " Jaz-Min said proudly from behind her king.

"Forgive her for speaking without your permission. She's still young and forgets the rules of your consent," the mathematician said in her defense.

"She has my permission to speak as she wishes," the king said.

"He's also the designer of this palace," Jaz-Min added as she heard the king giving her permission to speak again.

"Is that true old man? Speak now!

"Yes, great king. I was one of many who work to build this palace. Yes. You could say I was an architect then; it was in the time your grandfather. Your father then also only a young man," the old mathematician answered. The king remained standing and gazing at the old man. Thinking while the old mathematician stood, waiting for the king.

"Are those your charts under your arms? Have you figured out when and where the talking camel's door will open? The king asked pointing to the scrolls.

"Well, not exactly. Indeed nobody knows. But over the years my calculation points to one place. There is only one place that might be, but this is only my humble estimation and guess," my great king the old man answered.

The King's eyes flickered with attention again.

"Tell me now then. Don't make me more impatient old man," the king threatened.

Chapter Nineteen
Grant Me One Wish

"My daughter and my science are the love of my life. Just grant me one wish," asked the old mathematician looking directly at the king's eyes and bowing his head with respect for the ruler.

"And what would that wish be? Don't try my patience," the king said this time.

"That you free my only daughter. That you promise for your kingdom to let her return to me if my calculations please you, and I undo the camel's riddle," the old mathematician requested.

The king pondered about the old man's proposition. Then, he paced for a moment. He looked everywhere and nowhere for some time. He spoke again.

"Fine, be it like you ask. Very well then, as you wish it will be done, old man. I'll free your daughter. I'll pay you the reward offered for solving the riddle. And you'll return to my court and be our mathematician again if you wish that too. That is if your estimations are correct. But if you're wrong! The king paused. "Your daughter will remain in service of this palace. You won't see her again. And you will live forever in my darkest dungeon. Forever! The king's threatened the old mathematician. The old mathematician face paled. He loved his daughter more than anything in his life. She was more precious than gold and all gems.

He loved her more than his own life and he wished the king had asked for his head instead. Losing his only daughter, he could never stand, the old wise man said to himself with great sadness.

"Well, what do you want to say to me," the king asked impatiently.

"I shall find the camel's door and undo the camel's riddle too," the mathematician said. He worked many calculations in his head.

"I promise today and hear me you all my maids and servants of my court this oath I say.

"I the king of Egypt today I promise this mathematician today. I will full fill my oath to him for I am the king of Egypt," the King said loud for all to hear.

"I have a petition to make. I request to talk to every servant. All who heard the story of the beggar and the talking camel," the old mathematician asked the king.

The King clapped his hands. Every servant was commanded to come to the old mathematician. A day later or so, the wise old man had spoken to every one of the servants. The old mathematician relayed to the King what he learned from the servants. Many said the camel was white and as a cloud and he could fly. Others said he said the camel was tall and fat and many men the king would need to drag the camel with them. And so, the story went on and on. By the time the all finished saying what they heard, the camel was ten feet tall, his coat was of many colors and snout the largest snout ever.

But in the end, the old mathematician knew what he was looking for and he put all the rumors together and dismissed them all. "Humm, where do I begin? The mathematician said to himself as he stroked his beard.

"What is it now? The king asked in a bad mood for he was an impatient ruler.

"The camel must be in the last year of his life. His coat is getting older. It's losing its color. He's wandered close to five years in his own time in the desert. This means many years. It must reach the door or it will die," said the mathematician.

"What else? Don't speak to me in riddles and explain, "demanded the King again. The mathematician needed to be careful. He wanted to choose the right words.

He would lose his daughter if he was wrong and end in a dark dungeon too. But remembering something he had written many years before, he said I know, I know.

"It's a riddle written by my hand on a corner of an old scroll I found it. Let me read this for you this conundrum. For all you who can see without seeing. For those who hear without their ears, but your heart. Use your mind. Use your imagination for a short moment of your life. See without your eyes. You will find what you want. I have something that might help us to undo the ancient camel's riddle nobody knows how to read. But I need to talk to the children in this palace.

"So, be it," the king said impatiently and clapped his hand one more time. The old mathematician rehearsed the riddle in his mind and said it to himself for the umpteenth time. Uhmmm, he read:

"When the sun grows older and hides behind the great river. A pyramid shall cast its shadows over the land of the Pharaohs. Look no more. Stop and look beyond here and there. This and that your eyes may see. Its secret is there!

"A girl and a boy are kind and brave. Both siblings are from a cold land! His hair golden nugget is his; hers like iron on fire will be.

They'll find the door. They're both kind and brave indeed but both not from afar and will not look like other children in this kingdom! In the shadows, they will see the camel's passage at once. Measure the distance from the Death Sea and much more! It goes from there to the river that flows in front of Thee. Look at the moon.

"Its light will fall over the three Triangles. Follow the waters to the hidden door from the longest river. Look at the many angles and the casting of their shadows. Look at the moon and the light along the mighty Pyramid. Look at each side for it was built by the Pharaohs in front of Thee. Five years make only one. The last day is the key to this riddle.

One day and one month to the door will be on the five years but is one. Read, read, read; he who reads well the riddle, the door will find for Thee. Uhmm," the old mathematician said again to himself pondering.

The king got impatient again. The mathematician went on to say. "I've read this riddle a thousand times. It has been chanted and repeated a million more. And only now I think to have a possible answer. I've stopped believing in the Talking Camel even as a child. The science of men has blinded me. Only those who believe, like children," he said to himself, could undo the riddle.

He knew then what to do. He asked the king to gather all the children in the king's palace as he said before. He asked to bring the children to him. The king's five children were gathered in front of the old mathematician. He sat and asked the children to sit around him too. He read the riddle to each of the children. Each offered an answer to the riddle. One by one, the answers flowed from the children's mouths.

The pyramids of Giza were, of course, the three triangles in the land of the Pharaohs, one of the children said. The river in Front of Thee is the Nile river flowing through not far from the city to the Death Sea, the second child guessed correctly. It would take one month and one day to arrive from Cairo to Giza, the third child guessed too. Traveling measured by days on the river total exactly thirty days and one day, the fourth child said and he was correct.

The most precious clue came from the mouth of the littlest of the boys. He had been born in a leap year. Even five years old, he still was only one. When was asked how old he was, he said.

My mom says I was born five years ago, but even I'll be five my many years only count for one! The door would close, of course on the last days of the month, or five days from now.

Then, he babbled the answers as he walked to the king to tell him all about.

"I have the answer and I've not failed you, great king. But I'm afraid time is not our side. The camel's door will open on the largest of the pyramids of Giza. It will on any of its angles.
"Every day of this month when the full moonlight falls over it, "the old mathematician said with confidence.

"And why are you so worried then. Explain to me now." The king demanded.

"But your king there only a couple of days left for the door. Even your fastest horses would never reach Giza at full trot, "the mathematician said and went on. "At the last seven moons, a sign will come to the camel to see the door," he said.

The king gave orders to seek and find the camel before the signs were gone. One hundred of his men got ready to go. All men would be riding the fastest of their horses. Then, they all left galloping at a full trot to find the camel and the children.

"You will travel with me," the king said pointing a finger at the mathematician.

Chapter Twenty
The Grand Garden

"I come from afar, a faraway place named the Grand Garden, "said Tal-Mishem with a soft voice filled with nostalgia and perhaps many memories. "Its valleys are always covered with green, fresh pasture and the rivers run everywhere and without end, Tal-Mishem added.

"It is a place I should have never left, but like many others of my age, I ventured into the unknown. I passed the door to the humans' world," Tal-Mishem said as if speaking to himself.

"What door? Sarah asked curiously.

"A door that we have to find soon if we want him to go back to his family again, "Peter said to Sarah before TM.

"Do you know where to look for the door? Sarah asked alarmed.

"When the signs come I'll know where to look for the door Sarah but let me finish how my trip began for now," Tal-Mishem said and went to say more. "For many years as I got older my parents warned me about a door. A door that opens and one can travel to many worlds. But like many others before me, I didn't listen. I was curious perhaps and maybe disobedient too. I wanted to know it all. That is when my adventure really begins. I wanted to see other worlds.

"I got in trouble like that," Tal-Mishem said as if not believing he had made the same mistake as other youngsters. "I wanted to know others of my own kind in far nations. One day, against my parents' wishes I followed other voices," Tal-Mishem said recounting his trip. He paused.

"Please tell us more. What happened then? Sarah asked again.

"Well, other young camels like me, had gone and returned from many places. I thought also about all those wonders. I wanted to see them. I left my world through the door and ended here," Tal-Mishem said.

"You know exactly where and when the door may open," asked Peter worried.

"Well, it's a door no human can see. It opens only once every five years and the last month of every leap year only while the full moon shines. At the end of the full moon, it closes again. It does not open until five years later, "Tal-Mishem explained.

Peter didn't dare to ask fearing the interruption would stop TalMishem from recounting his story. Sarah wanted to know what a leap year was but waited. Tal-Mishem explained patiently that a leap year only occurred every five years and it had an extra day according to the celestial order of the planets.

"Where was I? Tal-Mishem asked wanting to continue.

"When you were saying you had left through the door, " Sarah reminded him.

"Oh, yes. Once a camel goes through the door it may only go back if he fills a mission in his destiny," Tal-Mishem paused. "Each camel and each animal that is part of the Universal creation has a destiny to full fill. A mission let's call it for now. One does a mission in life in different manners," added Tal-Mishem seeing the children's faces and went on.

"I needed to do a good deed before I can find the door and go back," Tal-Mashem said.

"You did, you helped us escape, right? "What's a good deed? Asked Sarah.

"You do something out of the goodness of your heart Sarah. Remember when you helped Smoochy your little dog?

"Yes, I helped not to feel pain," said Sarah.

"I know Sarah. I know you did that and believe me that is a good deed too. You also loved Smoochy and that was a good deed; being kind even to animals is a good deed, Sarah," said Tal-Mishem, his honey-brown walnut eyes on hers.

"Well, now that you know how camels fill their destinies, let us continue, "Tal-Mishem said.

"Our world is the Grand Garden. We're kind to each. It's like a rule we all followed. We camels in the Grand Garden own all. Everything is ours and nothing at the same time.

Do children live there too? Asked Sarah.

No Sarah, it's a world for animals only; all animals live like friends; we never hurt each other but the most important rule is Selfgovernment."

"What's that? Peter asked this time. "Each of us has received enough instruction about our free will.

One must think about the freedom of others and respect that as well. That is a universal law. It's in our hearts from the beginning of the universe," Tal-Mishem said.

'Are you going to be a king someday TM? Asked Sarah.

Maybe someday Sarah. I'm a prince now," Tal-Mishem said.

"Then you have many soldiers for war and go to battles, right? added Peters.

"We have no wars as many humans do. We don't have wars, Peter, never," Tal-Mishem said.

Do you have a family? Sarah asked, her eyes glowing with curiosity.

We have moms and dads, and grandpa-camels too. We love and respect the old and weak. Mothers of baby camels are honored for their motherhood. Only female camels can give life to others. Our children are the heirs to our wisdom and love. They're our future," Tal-Mishem said and paused.

"Can we come to visit your world? Sarah asked innocently.

"Perhaps someday Sarah; don't know when. These are some of the ways of our world. Each of us loves our family very much. We all have a mission.

Perhaps my mission was to come and meet you here. Every step we take in life takes us to our final home," Tal-Mishem said.

Then Tal-Mishem said, "As all creations, we have a path to follow and many steps ahead of us. Some are easy, others are not. It's a walk that may lead us in the right direction; but, sometimes in the wrong direction too. Nobody knows for sure where that trip begins. Or where it ends, but we'll get know at our final destination, "Tal-Mishem said.

Chapter Twenty-One
Final Home

Tal-Mishem waited for Peter and Sarah to think of something they wanted to ask. "Is this the road to our final destination? Peter asked. "It could be for me Peter, but not for you and Sarah yet. Your parents are seeking for you. Soon they're going to find you. Is it that what you two have wished for? That will be your wish number one for each of you," said Tal-Mishem.

Peter and Sarah rejoiced when hearing they would be with their parents soon, but Sarah had a million questions in her head fro TalMishem.

"How old are you TM, are very old? Sarah asked.

"Uhmm, that's a tricky one! Well, let me think here. I'm confused now with my age on this planet. He pondered mumbling to himself. If I multiply by one thousand and then I add this and those years. Let me see, wait; If I divide by three hundred and sixty-five years and minus five hundred years traveling. Well, more or less, I think possibly over one hundred years old. I am still a young lad, a young fellow, a young bloke or chap! As they say here," Tal-Mishem said and both Peter and Sarah laughed.

"Wow...Tal-Mishem then your destiny must very long too. Can we go back to the start of our destiny," Peter asked.

"I don't know Peter, but it's important we all walk in the right direction. My parents always told me. I should have listened to them. A perilous road may begin with small wrong step in the wrong direction," Tal-Mishem admitted.

"Is the Grand Garden far from London, Tal-Mishem? Asked Sarah thinking about England that was far too.

"Ah...Sarah, I come from afar, very far a place. But I don't know how to explain it. I'm not a mathematician yet, but one day I'm going to be one too," Tal-Mishem said.

In the meantime, the very same day that Peter and the children had left for the desert, the king of Egypt gathered all his men and ordered them to find the "Talking Camel". For years he had heard about the camel and the tales behind the story. He had spent many years and much of his energy looking for the talking camel. As a boy, he had dreamed like many others and finding the camel.

Once on his horse, he trotted at the head of his men. He pushed his own horse to run and never rested. But Tal-Mishem and the children were too far for the king to capture them. The door on the largest of the three pyramids, the pyramid of Giza, waited for Tal-Mishem.

On the first night, the king ordered his men to keep galloping after Tal-Mishem and the children. But on the third night, his men and their horses got tired. They needed rest and water. Still hiding in the old abandoned house Tal-Mishem rested getting ready for the last leg of their trip. His legs, he said, felt tired and heavier than ever from the last days of traveling. This time he wanted to ask the children to walk instead of riding on his back. How can I ask them? They're only small children and will get tired soon. I cannot do that, he thought, he told himself. Then, he heard Peter and Sarah asking to be granted their second wish.

"Tal-Mishem before we depart again, please grant us the wish to walk as far as we want to without ever, ever getting tired, "Peter said and Sarah thought that a good idea too.

"Granted, said Tal-Mishem looking at Peter and Sarah. His heart filled with love for them. Remember what I was telling you about our destiny. How we reach our final destination. We take our roadway to our future with every step we take now, "said Tal-Mishem while the children cuddle on his body.

"Yeah," Peter said. Sarah echoed him saying yes too.

"Sometimes the last steps are hard. One can get tired and sometimes is painful," Tal-Mishem said preparing the hearts of the children.

"Are we getting to the end of destination Tal-Mishem, " asked Peter and looked at the large, honey-brown eyes of Tal-Mishem fixed on him and Sarah. A tear had rolled down from the camel's eye to his snout.

"Well, maybe I'm beginning to feel tired," Tal-Mishem said resting his snout on the dirt floor and closing his eyes.

"Tal-Mishem?

"Yes Sarah, what is it?

"Are you missing your mom too? Sarah asked in a whisper.

"Yeah, I do so much like you now Sarah. But soon you and I and Peter are going to be with those we love. Believe me, Sarah, very soon. We're getting closer to them as we speak now," Tal-Mishem said to Sarah.

Then, Tal-Mishem thought about three triangles in the distance. They rose into the darkness of the night. Above the three pyramids, millions of stars showed up in the sky. The bluish light of the moon shone on them. The pyramids didn't look far but Tal-Mishem knew its life on earth was coming to its end. The door was too far from him perhaps. He told himself. How to tell the children Tal-Mishem thought. His body was getting weaker and weaker. Then, suddenly the ground beneath them rumbled!!

Tal-Mishem placed its head to the ground. He heard the galloping of many horses at full trot. The king horses only a short distance from them. They're coming, he thought.

"Peter and Sarah...wake up...wake up! The King and his men are coming for me now. They're coming for me. They aren't too far," TalMishem said alarmed and waited.

Then, the hoofing of horses pounding the ground grew louder and they all heard it clearly. Peter and Sarah cuddled closer to TalMishem for protection.

"They're here. They're looking for me. This is my final destination children, "Tal-Mishem said turning its head to Peter and Sarah.

"Tal-Mishem? Said Sarah.

"Yes, Sarah.

"Please grant us our last wishes," Sarah begged.

"Yes, anything Sarah, " Tal-Mishem said.

"I, said Sarah, wish for you to walk, find the door and go home. Can you grant me that wish?

"Yes, but you'll need your last wish to return home, " Tal-Mishem protested.

"I already asked my parents to find me, remember? They will find us for you granted us that wish too," Sarah said in her tiny voice.

"I, said Peter, want to make you invisible to the king's men. So, they cannot see you and you can walk in front of them like a king too," Peter wished.

At that very moment, the king's men walked into the abandoned barn looking for the talking camel and the children. The captain of the troops shouted.

"Here, mighty king. There are children hiding here!! The captain of the guards said. "But there is no camel here, great king. Only two foreign children," the man yelled. Peter and Sarah cuddled together in a corner of the old barn. Their brave hearts hoped their parents would come soon. Peter and Sarah looked around. Their eyes glowed with happiness. Tal-Mishem goodbye got into the children's heads.

Peter said, "dad is coming soon Sarah; be brave remember?

Sarah smiled. She knew too. She had wished that with all her heart and it was coming through as Tal-Mishem had promised her.

"Take them with you and bring them to me. They're coming with us! The king ordered

Chapter Twenty-Two
Tal-Mishem Goes Home

The King and his horsemen galloped all night. By daybreak arrived at Giza. The three pyramids indeed looked like giant triangles. Not too far from them the Nile river. Palm trees along the river gave shade to the people protecting them from the sun. It made the land rich with green endless pastures. People could grow grains anything they wanted and sell in their markets. They could make a living selling their harvests.

"Oh, the river Nile. I swam in it many times as a child, the king said remembering his happy childhood. The Nile is more real than any fantastic camel I want to have as a toy. No, I'm not a boy anymore. I'm a king now, "the king said in a whisper turning his head for the mathematician to hear.

"Yes, I remembered well. We came many times to see you play and swim here," the mathematician said.

And he said aloud. "I came here as a child-prince and plunged into the river many times.

"I had many friends and family then. I was very happy as a child, "the king said. He remembered how happy he had been as a child and not as the king of Egypt. He missed his family and friends. I forgot about all this wanting the Talking Camel only for me! The king said.

The old mathematician said, "It's too late now. The camel is gone. Before your father's father and other kings before them; the White Talking Camel come only to children who needed him.

"Maybe it was never for me. He's a free camel as I'm a free man," the king said.

"Let it be, mighty king, let it be. Your kingdom waits for you. Your people are going to look up to a wise king.

"You could be that king for them. Perhaps it's time for the mighty king to forget all this nonsense. Instead, a family could bring you happiness.

Be good and just king also. Remember the many slaves that labor in your kingdom too; perhaps you would want to be kind and let go free. They suffer, their families too. That would make many your loyal friends again for nobody before you have made them free men."

"Your words are wise and good counsel to my heart and ears," the king said listening.

"Yes, yes, the camel, it runs from here to there and everywhere, but nobody had ever seen this camel. Perhaps the whole thing is only a bed story for children. Maybe it was meant to be always a free camel and not a toy in the gardens of your palace," the wise man said.

"Like many other children I dreamed about the riding on its loins and fly with him," the king said.

"I did too believe in him as a kid, I believed too like you, mighty king. I wanted to see him even for one moment. I went looking everywhere for the king of camels, the camel king, the White Talking Camel.

"We dreamed like children dream, even you perhaps wise old man," the king said.

"Oh, yes, indeed, great king, I did, but one day I heard myself saying "let it be, if he wants to, he will one day come to thee. I instead learned how to read and write well, then I studied the stars and the galaxies. I became a mathematician instead and here I'm," the wise mathematician added hoping to convince the king to forget about the camel and a just king instead.

"Very wise if you, old man," the king said.

"Then, I built palaces and gardens for our kings.
"In time, I earned the respect of many kings, found a wife and a family, and Jaz-Min came to be my daughter and lived happily since then," the mathematician said with a grin in his face.

"You're a wise old mathematician. Yes, I've spent too much time looking for the camel king indeed. I've managed the affairs of my kingdom poorly. I've forgotten to be a just king and make my people happy. There are beggars on the streets. There are thieves in the mountains. There are hungry people on the streets. Too many of our young warriors have gone out to war too far lands way too many times.

What have I done to make my people happy? It's a shame on me, old mathematician; shame on me, for many years, the king added with regret.

"Understanding your many wrong paths, may one lead us to the right one," my king the mathematician said.

"Yes, indeed, But I promise you to be a new king from now on. I shall govern my kingdom with wisdom. I shall govern my kingdom with kind and justice from now on. I will stop having slaves in my kingdom and every man will be free from now on, "the kind said. It will make your kingdom prosperous and happy," the old man commented.

"And, I shall look for a queen to be my wife forever. I will ask her for children to love and care for and be a family. I will seek to have my own family and be happy again, "the king said.

"My heart fills with happiness to hear our mighty king. He's thinking to be a new man. A just king to the people he commands. For sure the people will come to respect you.

That will make your kingdom a peaceful nation to live in and people know of your wisdom and will come to be your people, "the mathematician said sincerely for the king's ears and heart.

Twenty-Three
A New King –

"Very well then, a new king I will be from this day on. I'll begin with honoring my oath to you. You guessed right the camel's riddle. Your daughter's freedom you will have today and now, "the king said.

The old mathematician's heart filled with happiness again. He was sad thinking the king could break his promise. That he could keep his daughter against her will in his palace. The old mathematicians now had only one worry.

He needed to ask the king now that he wanted to be a just ruler. And he did ask again.

"Are the children we're holding our prisoners just king? "the mathematician asked.

"Of course not, no, they're free to go. I will ask you to look after them. Also, call the English ambassador and return them to their parents, "the king said to his now court mathematician.

"Oh, mighty king, it pleases me and I accept. I'll look upon the children's welfare while in the palace. Perhaps my daughter Jaz-Min may help me. She could look after them when my duties are too many," said the mathematician.

"It pleases me too that you have thought of Jaz-Min to attend these children. She's free to do as she is pleased from this day on. Be it known to all in my kingdom. I've kept my oath to you. But I have a request to ask from you wise man," the king said.

"Please tell me, my king, what that request might be," the wise man asked.

"Uhmm....your daughter is free to go. But it would please me very much if she remains in my kingdom with you," the king said.

"And why is that mighty King? How could she serve you more than I can?

"She is only a young maid with limited instruction. It's not her fault though. She's intelligent and loves numbers like your humble servant, me, "the old mathematician asked.

'Uhmmm..." the king cleared his voice and said, "I find her most sincere. Her beauty pleases me very much. I would like to ask you for her hand. Marry her to be my only wife and queen of my kingdom," the king said as he looked at his father-in-law to be.

The old mathematician smiled at the king and granted his daughter's hand to the king of Egypt.

"It would be my honor, my king for she is the love of my heart, "the new mathematician to the Egyptian court said with pride.

In the meantime, Peter heard voices filling his head. He held the giggling marbles in his hand. He heard them again.

"Peteeeerrrr! He heard his name called out. It was his mother's voice. Her voice sounded very distant at first. It was too far to be heard well. Then, he heard his father's voice too shouting their names. The voices louder and louder, he thought perhaps getting closer with the wind coming their way.

"Here! mom…here dad..! Both children shouted happily. The children cried out for help. Their mental message flew to their parents too. Minutes later a cloud of dust coming their way showed at the distance.

"Peteeeerrrr and Saraaaaaaaaah! Their parents' voices heard clearly in their minds.

"Your parents are coming. I have to go now. But I'll see you soon," Tal-Mishem said in a soft whisper fading away.

The English soldiers stopped. They greeted the king. At the head of the royal troops were the children's parents. They were announced to the king. A handful of English soldiers from the royal crown stood behind them.

The captain of the king introduced the English envoy. An official from royal English crown and he said, "Mr. Maxwell Carnerhill ambassador for England in Egypt and Mrs. Carnerhill his wife are parents of these children. Then, both parents dismounted from their horses.

They ran to their children. They hugged them and kissed them. Tears falling from their eyes for their hearts had filled with happiness again. They have missed them very much. They've gone everywhere looking for them.

Days and weeks had passed from the day of their kidnap. Sarah embraced her mom saying, "I missed you so very much mom. I'm not afraid of camels anymore. You know the white talking camel is brave and kind too. He even talks, mom, "Sarah said. Her mother smiled at her. She understood. she ran to her dad to tell him that too and tell him she loved him
very much. "We've also missed you very much, "her mom said to her in a whisper.

Dad, mom! Peter said, "believe me, we have something to tell you. It's about this camel. He roams the desert. He's a white talking camel and he came to help us. He's gone now! Believe me dad, and mom. He roams the desert from here to there and then everywhere! Nobody can see him! Some people say he even flies sometimes. His coat turns white and it glows at night. It turns yellow or any color if he wants to hide. He's also a king for his own kind and in his own constellation, Dad and mom.

"Believe it, he's tall and strong. He's smart and talks in many languages. If you came across him and you could see him. He's fantastic!!

"He would talk to you in English and French, or Portuguese and Spanish. Even mentally and you would understand him. He's very smart too. He knows of numbers and faraway stars, believe me. If he were human, he would be a prince or king for sure. He's kind and brave! Peter said from his heart.

Their parents were glad the camel had helped them to escape. They winked an eye to each other. Peter hugged her mom and his dad one more time. Then, together they all hugged again. Peter and Sarah followed their parents. Horses waited for them to travel back to Cairo.

"Common children. We're going home!! Their mother called out.

"You're going home, Peter and Sarah!

We're all going where we belong!! Tal-Mishem said as he traveled home to millions of miles away. His mental goodbye got to the children. Both Peter and Sarah heard him and smiled. Peter closed his fingers over the magic marble in his pocket and asked.

"Sarah, did you hear that? Sarah closed her finger over the giggler marble in her hand too and said, "Goodbye Tal-Mishem. I'll miss you too. See you soon PAUL-MISHEM!! She said and giggled. What did you call him..??

"I like Paul better than Tal. It's a secret between him and me," Sarah said and giggled again.

The king raised his hand along with his mathematician saying goodbye too. The king then said, "the White Talking Camel they've seen for they've indeed believed! For they are brave of heart and kind children indeed!

THE END